RANCHER TO THE RESCUE

BARB HAN

TORJAKE PUBLISHING

Editing: Ali Williams

Cover Design: Jacob's Cover Designs

To my family for unwavering love and support. I can't imagine doing life with anyone else. I love you guys with all my heart.

1

The first day of June in South Central Texas had been without a cloud in sight, a rare occurrence. Thunderstorms were known to light up the skies and dump water on the earth out of seemingly nowhere this time of year, though the recent drought promised they wouldn't any time soon.

Adam Firebrand stood on the edge of Angel Pass, staring out across the land he loved. After yesterday's news, he couldn't help but be reminded of how fragile it all was and, just like the sky, how quickly everything could change.

As if Mother Nature could hear his thoughts, a cloud rolled in and a light sprinkle dusted his face. He stood there anyway, taking it all in.

Firebrands had been standing on this land for three generations before him and had weathered a lot of storms in the process. Bad luck didn't discriminate, and they'd had their fair share even though few families had done better financially. Their successful cattle ranch extended as far as the naked eye could see.

Now that the Marshall had died, the fate of their family

legacy was up in the air. Adam had no idea what to expect from his grandfather's last will and testament. The two of them weren't exactly two peas in a pod. But then no one got close to Marshall Firebrand, so Adam had never taken the snub personally.

His grandfather had, however, stoked the fire between his sons at every turn. Two brothers had never fought so hard or so often as Adam's father and uncle, Brodie and Keifer.

Case in point, the Marshall hadn't been buried yet, and Adam's father and uncle were already in a lather over the will. All Adam knew for certain was that neither his father nor his uncle seemed pleased when he'd passed them in the kitchen at the main house last night. Not one of their combined eighteen sons had been invited to the meeting with the family lawyer either. His mother wasn't saying much, which was most definitely a bad sign. Another look at both of them this morning said all Adam needed to know. The Marshall had pulled something. So Adam was in no hurry to get back to the main house.

Only half of his brothers and cousins worked the successful cattle ranch and they'd been in a mood this morning at the barn too. The ones who were out of town or overseas had been notified of the Marshall's passing, so Adam figured it was only a matter of time before each made their way home to pay respects. No matter how much of an old grouch their grandfather had been, the guys would honor tradition. Once a Cowboy Code was ingrained in a person, the ideals weren't easily shed. No matter how much Firebrands might disagree with each other, they followed the same ideals.

What should be a green field in front of him was plagued with brown patches, thanks to twin years of drought-like conditions. Looking onto the vista that was normally nothing but miles of green hills dotted with bluebonnets, he realized how interdependent nature was. Family bonds were no different. Much less had ripped them apart forever. He would hate for the precious land and cattle to get caught up in a legal battle. Not to mention the fact that Adam's father and uncle were gasoline on fire anytime they were in the same room. All it took was one match to devastate the countryside.

He shook his head and made a tsk-tsk sound. The Firebrands had stubborn streaks a mile long, which wasn't going to help. Heels would be dug in. Lines would be drawn. All bets would be off for the family who hadn't been able to get together for a Sunday barbeque in more years than Adam cared to count. And that was under the best circumstances.

Despite practically dripping sweat from nearly fifteen hours straight of repairing fences, Adam wasn't quite ready to call it a day. His stomach growled, reminding him how long it had been since lunch. He'd eaten a power bar to get him through to supper, but the energy from that was wearing thin. The barn was half an hour ride from Angel Pass on horseback. While most ranching operations had moved to using trucks to move cattle and ATVs to run fences, Adam still rode horseback. Call him a renaissance man, but it was the only way to go in his book.

Besides, Luna needed the exercise and there wasn't much better than spending a day out here with his Appaloosa by his side. She was all the company he needed. Hell, she was the only one he'd spent any amount of time with since Libby refused his proposal and walked out of his life. What was it with the first of June bringing events that wreaked havoc on his life?

He'd been blaming his mood on the fact he'd lost his

grandfather. Did it also have something to do with this being the ten-month anniversary of losing the woman he'd been intent on spending the rest of his life with?

He'd adored her. Too bad she hadn't felt the same. Or was it? He couldn't help but think he'd dodged a bullet now. There was no way he wanted to spend the rest of his life with someone whose *I love you* meant something totally different than his.

Lost in thought, Adam couldn't be sure how long he'd been standing there when he heard the first noise. It sounded a whole lot like a baby's cry. But that didn't make sense out here.

He shook his head and cleaned out the earwax. He couldn't possibly be hearing right. Maybe there was a small animal in trouble. None of the ranch hands would be on this stretch of land and Bronc, the foreman, had claimed the west side of the property in the meeting this morning. Plus, the fact they were all grown men while the sound he kept hearing mimicked a baby.

Could the wind to his back carry a noise all the way up here at Angel Pass? He doubted it even though the winds had kicked up a few notches as more clouds rolled in overhead. The light mist had dried up, which was unfortunate given the ground conditions. They needed rain.

Again, the cry pierced the air.

Was he dehydrated? Hallucinating? It had happened once after a long, sweaty day when he hadn't kept up with his water. As luck would have it, his brother Brax happened to ride up in the nick of time. He'd saved Adam's life that day by picking him up and tossing him onto Luna's back. Brax had brought horse and rider home on that ground-cracking day.

Adam had barely passed his twentieth birthday at the

time and had gotten cocky, thinking he could outlast the late-August heat. From then on, though, Adam respected the elements. Lesson learned.

The baby wailed. The desperate quality got Adam's feet moving toward his horse. He hopped into Luna's saddle and backtracked toward the noise coming from a patch of trees. He was an expert tracker since poachers were a threat to cattle ranches, but he didn't need to call on any of his experience. All he had to do was follow the sound of the baby, who hadn't stopped crying since Adam first heard the sound.

Despite the urgency in the baby's voice, Adam doubted there was any real crisis here. Babies sent up the alarm for various reasons, one of which was hunger. He'd seen a kid throw a full-on temper tantrum at the feed store once because he didn't want to put on his coat in the dead of winter. Negotiating didn't seem to do any good either. The parent got so flustered she threw her hands up and walked the little tyke outside and into the cold in his t-shirt.

Adam had very little experience around kids, and no desire to add to his resume. Libby had put the nail in that coffin. Now, he was content to date around and keep his options open. An annoying voice in the back of his mind picked that moment to remind he should get started on that liberated lifestyle instead of licking his wounds over his loss. It had almost been a year.

Thoughts raced through his mind as to what could be going on with the kiddo. It was highly possible a family was out here, lost. Campers who might not realize they'd wandered onto private land. No one dangerous like poachers would bring a baby along. They traveled incognito. He wasn't worried about coming up on anything dangerous, so he didn't try to hide his presence. Instead, he started whistling, though he doubted anyone could hear him over the baby's racket. He'd also learned it wasn't good to surprise people who normally carried some type of weapon on camping trips.

This was going to be a simple case of explaining the rules about being on private property. Someone probably needed an escort in order to find their way off the land. Adam was protective over his family's legacy, and he didn't mind helping folks out. It would be nightfall soon and there were all manner of wild animals on ranch property.

As the noise escalated, he couldn't help but wonder why someone hadn't been able to pacify the kid. Was it sick? Hungry?

The Good Samaritan feeling spread inside him. He was about to bail someone out of trouble, someone who had a family. And then an uneasy feeling followed, taking hold in the pit of his stomach as he neared.

The trees in his area were thicker. The scrub brush higher. Rather than risk Luna twisting an ankle, Adam hopped down and tied her to a tree so she wouldn't get tangled in her own reins. He'd made that mistake in his youth too. He'd covered pretty much all of them in his thirty-eight years on the planet. The biggest one had been waiting to get married. He'd convinced himself Libby was different, special.

Adam changed the subject before he choked on the irony.

"Hello?" he shouted, trying to out scream the baby so he wouldn't catch its caregiver off guard. Surprise out in these parts could be deadly.

From around a tree, the most intense set of blue eyes peered at him. Wheat-colored hair slicked back in a bun and Coke-rimmed glasses didn't give the unfamiliar face away. Her full lips weren't something he needed to focus on, so he forced his gaze to the pink bundle with a set of lungs in her arms.

"Help," Blue Eyes said. The one word spoken in such an anxious voice, tightened the knot that had formed in Adam's gut. She opened her left hand and a sharp stick tumbled out.

So much for desperate.

$\sim$

PRUDENCE OWENS STARED into the most intense and beautiful pair of eyes she'd ever seen. "I'm Prudence."

"Adam," he said but she already knew his name. "What are you doing out here?"

He had every right to ask the question and she wished she had an answer for him. All she could do was shrug.

Adam had been five or six grades ahead of Prudence in school, so she knew him by name and reputation only. She'd been in the same grade as his younger brother Fallon, though she hadn't known him personally either. It seemed like the Firebrands were all sports stars or popular kids, whereas as she would have been voted most likely to be found in the library.

He shot her a look of disbelief.

"I have no idea. I promise." Prudence wasn't lying. She couldn't for the life of her remember much of anything that had happened today or how she'd ended up with this angel in her arms. She glanced down at the bundle. "I don't know what she wants. Can you please help?"

"Not sure what I can do," he said, his words spoken with the same hopelessness she felt. "Do you have a bottle? Milk? Some sort of bag to carry diapers in?"

"No. None of those things," she admitted, as panic made it hard to breathe. Panic she had no intention of giving into, despite the tight feeling in her chest.

Adam offered a hand up. She took it, ignoring the jolt of electricity that came with contact. He met her gaze and held a second longer than she figured was appropriate. Was he studying her? Trying to figure out if she was mentally unstable or a baby thief?

"How did you get out here?" Adam studied the area like it was midterms, and he was trying to pass English.

"I already said that I have no idea." The baby's cries literally caused Prudence's heart to ache. "Any chance we can figure all that out after we find a way to feed her? She must be starving since she keeps trying to suck on her fist."

Adam locked gazes for a long moment. A squirrel got loose in her stomach.

"I promise to explain everything once she's settled." It was a deal Prudence knew she couldn't make good on. She couldn't afford to feel bad about fudging the truth while the baby was suffering.

"Luna is nearby," Adam said.

"Let's go." Prudence wasted no time moving in the direction of what she figured must be his horse. Luna would be an unusual name for a truck.

He led her to a gorgeous Appaloosa.

"I can hold her while you climb in the saddle." He motioned toward the baby.

Prudence shook her head, unsure why she refused the offer. She searched her brain for an answer and came up empty. All she knew was this baby would have to be pried out of her hands. "Can you pick me up? I'd rather hold onto her."

Adam was as strong as an ox. He managed to lift her up

like she weighed nothing. Both hands on her waist, he hoisted her high enough for her to throw a leg over the animal's back without further disturbing the little girl.

He was in the saddle a moment later and they were headed toward salvation.

Halfway through the ride, the little angel found her fist again, stuffing it in her mouth and sucking. The calm respite did little to slow Prudence's galloping heart. It was impossible to think clearly with Adam's strong arms wrapped around her, securing her and the child in the saddle.

Luna carried them to the steps of the back porch of an impressive house. The two-story brick and stone home was the biggest Prudence had ever seen. Grand wasn't quite big enough a word to describe the exterior, but it was a good place to start. Charm was another word that didn't quite do it justice. And yet, it *was* charming. They'd already ridden past an impressive set of barns, which was where she began to notice the place had everything in pairs. She made a mental note to ask about that later. Right now, all she could focus on was finding a bottle and...what?...milk?

One of Adam's brothers came bolting out of the house with a concerned look on his face.

"What's going on?" he asked. "Bronc phoned when he saw you."

"Brax, have you met Prudence?" Adam asked as he hopped off the horse.

Brax shook his head before tipping his hat by way of introduction. "What can I do to help?"

"Take Luna to the barn. Make sure she's well cared for," Adam said. After that run, she would be lathered up. He turned to Prudence. "Lean toward me."

She did and he caught her. More of that electricity coursed through her. She mentally shook it off.

"I'll take care of Luna myself," Brax said, taking the reins. It was obvious the brothers were close. It also seemed to be understood Brax would be filled in later.

Adam seemed to thank his brother by way of a bear hug.

"Any chance we have baby's milk inside the house?" Adam asked. "Pantry?"

Brax shot a clueless look. "You got me."

"Thanks anyway, man," Adam said.

Brax nodded before heading toward the red barn. He shouted back, "Nice to meet you."

"Same." Prudence had passed him in town half a dozen times. This didn't seem like the time to bring it up. Plus, she had a way of blending into the woodwork when she wanted to. Crowds of people had never been her thing.

"This way." Adam held the door open for her. The man was sheer perfection with black as a night sky hair that was just long enough to curl. By contrast, his eyes were the palest blue and he had the thickest, longest lashes she'd ever seen. Make-up companies would kill to photograph them. Not to mention the man was six-feet-three-inches of solid muscle. He had the kind of cheekbones that looked good on a billboard with someone in their underwear and had the smokin' hot bod to pull it off, with just enough scruff on his face to be sexy and a set of the most piercing eyes.

Her throat dried up as she walked by him and onto the screened-in back porch, complete with flat-screen TV, a fireplace, and a sitting area larger than her entire house. If this was any indication of what she was about to walk into, she needed to take in a deep breath. And probably a few more for good measure.

Adam's cell buzzed. He fished it out of his pocket as he held the backdoor open for her. She walked into the kitchen that would be a professional chef's dream as he answered the call.

"Luna okay?" were the first words out of his mouth. His concern for his horse struck her in a deep place. He said a few uh-huhs into the phone before glancing at Prudence. "How old do you think the baby is?"

"No idea. She can't be too old. She doesn't have any teeth," Prudence supplied.

Again, Adam shot her a concerned look as he relayed the message. Shortly after, he ended the call.

"Brax gathered the ranch hands. Casey's wife just had a baby. He's bringing formula and supplies to the main house right now," Adam said. "In the meantime, do you want to tell me why it is you have a baby in your arms you seem to know nothing about?"

It was then Prudence remembered the piece of paper. She dug it out of her pocket, grateful the baby had momentarily gone to sleep sucking on her fist.

"I found this tucked inside her blanket." She held the wadded-up note on the flat of her palm.

When he took the offering, his fingers grazed her hand. Contact sent a sensual current skittering across her skin.

Adam flattened out the piece of paper on the granite center island. His pale blue eyes widened as he read the name: *Adam Firebrand*.

2

"Is this some kind of joke?" Adam stared at the paper with the same intensity as someone who was looking at a bomb about to detonate. His blank, frustrated glower gave the impression he had no idea why his name would be brought up.

"I don't know," Prudence said. Her defenses kicked into high gear. "I have no idea where the note came from."

"Then who does this baby belong to?" he asked. "She's clearly not yours and I've never seen her before."

Before she could answer, the screen door squeaked and then the back door flung open. Two men came charging in. Adam immediately introduced her to Casey and Bronc.

Casey, the younger of the two men, had a diaper bag slung over his shoulder. He sized the baby up. "She isn't more than a few weeks old. I'm guessing you don't know the formula she usually takes?" He glanced at Prudence.

She shook her head, wishing she could say something helpful.

"My son's will be better than nothing. She might get an upset stomach because the doc recommends sticking with the same kind, but we can deal with that when the time comes. Maybe we'll get lucky and this will be what she's used to." He went to work, laying out supplies before fixing and heating a bottle.

"His wife and son live with her mother in Henson Falls, which is a town over. He lives here at the bunkhouse during the week and goes home every other weekend," Adam whispered, his body strung tight.

In no time at all Casey produced a bottle. He tested the milk on the inside of his wrist. "This is the way my wife taught me to make sure it isn't too hot."

Prudence didn't know the first thing about caring for a baby. She appreciated all the advice she could get. Casey was straight from heaven.

"Any chance you have a diaper in the bag?" she asked.

"They might be too big for her, but yes," Casey said with a puzzled look on his face. He, like Adam, must be wondering why she had a baby she had no idea how to take care of. That was the baffling part. Prudence's mind was blank when it came to how it all went down. She knew for a fact the baby wasn't hers.

Casey guided the bottle right into the little girl's mouth, who rooted around for it the minute the nipple came close to her cheek. The timing was perfect because she'd run out of patience with her fist and was winding up to belt out her dissatisfaction with the whole situation.

She immediately started sucking, and settled down then, curling her fist up against her chest. Prudence's heart melted like butter sitting in the sun on a summer day. She looked at Casey. "Thank you so much."

"Much obliged, ma'am." Casey looked pleased with himself for being able to help.

"Why don't you sit down to feed the baby?" Adam motioned toward a table large enough to seat an army.

"Good idea. My feet are killing me." She had on her usual work outfit of sweats and a pair of tennis shoes.

"Can I get you something to drink?" Adam asked her before thanking Casey and Bronc.

"Water, if it's not too much trouble," she said, grateful for his consideration.

"We best be heading out," Bronc said. He looked to be in his late sixties with weather-worn skin and a permanent tan. His forehead seemed to have a permanent worry line etched into it. "Unless you need anything else."

"I think we have it under control from here," Adam said after a quick glance at Prudence.

"Okay then. We'll get out of your hair." Bronc looked to Prudence. "Ma'am."

She thanked him again.

"If you don't mind me saying…" Casey shifted his weight from foot to foot as he twisted the cowboy hat in his hands that he'd taken off after handing over the bag. "You're going to want to burp her after the bottle. Otherwise, she can get one heckuva stomach cramp. There's a towel in the front pocket that you put over your shoulder so she doesn't spit up on your clothes."

"Right. I'll be sure to do that." Prudence had plenty of experience with dogs and cats, thanks to her pet sitting service. She'd once taken care of a goat while a family vacationed, but she had limited experience with kids of the human variety. But spit up on this old shirt would blend in with the other smudges.

Bronc gave an awkward smile before he led the younger ranch hand out the back.

"Everything all right with them?" Prudence noted how

uncomfortable Bronc seemed and hoped it wasn't her fault. Despite living in Lone Star Pass her entire life, she'd only run into Bronc a handful of times and he had no reason to remember her. In fact, she blended into most backgrounds so much so the comment she heard from people the most was, *I didn't realize you still lived here.* She shouldn't be surprised, considering she kept to herself most of the time. The only folks she knew well enough to wave at were her clients.

Normally, thinking about being in town caused her chest to tighten and panic to set in. Not now. In fact, part of her wanted to march right down Main Street and say hello to everyone she passed. What was suddenly so different?

"Bronc doesn't think it's his place to be inside the main house," Adam said. "No amount of arguing has convinced him otherwise. He was the closest to our grandfather out of anyone, worked for my grandfather longer than I've been alive. What can I say? Bronc is old school. Between you and me, I don't think he likes having any sort of roof over his head." Adam fixed a glass of water, and then brought it over. He set it on the table beside her.

His demeanor had shifted, softening toward her. She couldn't help but wonder why. Was it because the baby had quieted down?

"Now, it's your turn," he said. She must've shot him a severe look because he quickly added, "First, to tell me why you have a piece of paper with my name on it. Then, to tell me what you're doing on my family's land with a baby you have no idea how to take care of and no supplies."

"Good questions," she said with a shrug.

"Are you running from someone?" His blunt question caught her off guard because it resonated.

"I'm not sure," she admitted. "I don't think so."

Her non-answer seemed to set him off. He stood there, fuming.

"I'm not trying to be evasive. I just don't have any memory of how I got here or how we ended up on your land. I apologize for tres—"

"Don't think anything else about it," Adam interjected, those serious pale blue eyes of his seemed to look right through her. "I'm just concerned for the welfare of you both."

"I appreciate it." Before she could ask him to call the sheriff, the bottle was drained and the baby was sucking on air. She pulled it out and the baby practically cooed in her sleep. Prudence hated to wake her, but the diaper was heavy and she needed to figure out how to burp the little angel. "Do you mind handing me the towel Casey mentioned?"

Adam rummaged in the front pocket of the diaper bag and came up with a padded hand towel.

She placed it over her shoulder, leaned forward with the baby, and then repositioned the sleeping angel so her head was on Prudence's shoulder. "I'm not sure how to do this."

Patting the baby's back didn't work.

"Try bouncing a little bit," Adam offered.

She did, and voila. His suggestion worked.

Pride filled her chest at having the baby fed, burped, and sleeping despite a wet diaper. "Where should I change her?"

"I felt something on the side of this thing." Adam reached for the diaper bag. He set it on the table next to them. He unsnapped one side and unfolded a mat. Something that looked a lot like pride passed behind his eyes when he said, "Try putting her on this."

Prudence stood, and then placed the baby on the makeshift changing table. All the supplies she needed were inside the bag; wipes, bottom cream, and a dozen or so diapers. There was also a binky and an assortment of plastic bottle inserts along with packets of formula. She suddenly realized she should have drilled Casey with questions while she had someone with experience in the room. It was clear both she and Adam were fumbling their way through the diaper change.

The diapers were a tad too big, the baby too small, but Prudence made it all work. More of that pride filled her chest at the accomplishment. She swaddled the baby in the blanket before returning to her seat.

"What should we do next?" she asked. "Call the sheriff and see if any babies have been reported missing?"

Adam palmed his cell. He stopped mid-dial. "Are you sure you have no idea why my name was in her blanket?"

"Afraid so," she said, not liking his frown at the non-answer. "My first thought, of course, was that you must be her father."

She'd clearly caught him off guard with that comment because his jaw nearly dropped all the way to the expensive tiled floor.

"I DON'T HAVE ANY CHILDREN." Adam would be the first to know if he did. "I'm not seeing anyone and haven't been for a long time."

"Then, maybe the person wrote down your name because he or she knew you would protect this little angel?" she surmised.

He'd had the exact same thought. Again, he drew a blank on who that might be. He studied the paper to see if he recognized the handwriting. Then again, he couldn't remember the last time someone had written him a note.

The letters were small, and it looked like they'd been hastily scribbled.

"I don't know anyone who is pregnant or has been in the past...for however many months it takes to brew one of those things...nine?" His question was rhetorical. He remembered something about nine months being a full-term pregnancy. If this kiddo was a few weeks old, it was mathematically impossible for the child to be his.

Someone had to be missing her.

He was more than mildly curious as to why Prudence was holding a child she didn't know. And didn't seem to have any memories of how the baby showed up. This situation definitely called for the law's intervention.

"That sounds right," Prudence said. She had the most interesting eyes hiding behind those Coke-bottle glasses.

"I'll get Sheriff Lawler on the line. See if we can figure out what happened. Someone will be missing a sweet little angel like her." He didn't see the need to mention the disturbing set of pipes the kid on her. They were strong.

Prudence nodded.

He picked up where he left off calling Lawler. Since poachers were a serious problem to ranchers, Adam had the lawman's number on speed dial.

"What can I do for you, Adam?" Timothy Lawler had been two grades ahead of Adam in school, so they knew of each other. Lawler had been a star quarterback who was being scouted by some big-name programs when he took a hit that broke his arm in four places. He'd managed to get off the game-winning throw, but the injury had ended his career and any hopes of playing college ball. He'd gone to school and studied criminal justice instead and then followed in his father's footsteps in law enforcement.

"Any chance you're looking for a few weeks' old baby?"

Adam had never been one to mince words. Now seemed like a bad time to start.

"No. Why?" Lawler had a shocked quality to his tone that was laced with disbelief, like he was about to ask if this was a prank.

"Prudence," he glanced at her drawing a blank on her last name.

"Owens," she supplied.

"Owens," he echoed, "is here with an infant and has no idea how she got her."

"Is Prudence hurt in any way?" Lawler's questions came without hesitation.

"She looks fine," he said before covering the mouthpiece. "Do you remember encountering anyone? Falling? Hitting your head on anything?"

"Nope. I'm drawing a blank on the whole of today," she admitted. Her cheeks heated with something that looked a lot like embarrassment.

He relayed the message to Lawler.

"Is the child okay?" Lawler asked.

"She looks healthy and just had a bottle that Casey brought up," he said adding, "I can verify her lungs are in full working condition."

This had to be one of those oddball situations that could be cleared up with a few phone calls. "There's no one looking for a newborn?"

"Afraid not. Hold on." The click-clack-clack of fingers on a keyboard came across the line. Then, quiet.

Adam didn't realize he'd started tapping the toe of his boot on the tile flooring.

"Nothing on my end," Lawler finally said. "I'll head on over."

Adam thanked the sheriff before ending the call and

turning to Prudence. "While we wait for the sheriff, why don't you tell me a little bit about yourself."

She cradled that baby like the infant would have to be pried out of her hands. He wondered if she even realized she was doing it. Was she a mother?

"There's not much to tell," she said. "I run a pet-sitting business." Something dawned on her because her face lit up. "I'm taking care of the Fritzes' dog while they're on vacation." She glanced down at her dark sweatpants. "That's why I have dog hair on me. I'd been out walking Henry."

It almost seemed like her memories were going to come flooding back. Her jaw clenched and her hand fisted before she issued a sigh. "Nope. Nothing. I only remember walking Henry."

Her face morphed from frustrated to determined.

"I have to get back to my job and take care of him," she said as a mix of panic and resolve washed over her features.

"Hold tight. What's the address to the Fritzes' house?" he asked. He should probably know except that he'd never been one to keep tabs on his neighbors or anyone else in town. He'd been too caught up in Libby during their relationship and then licking his wounds for the past year since the heartbreak to notice much of anything.

Prudence rattled it off.

"How about if I ask Bronc to go over and see to Henry while we wait for the sheriff here?" he asked, figuring Henry was probably just fine at home.

She seemed to think about it for a long moment. "I guess that could work. Would it be possible for him to stay with Henry until I get there? He gets anxious when he's left alone, and I have no idea how long I've been gone."

"I can ask, but I doubt there'll be any objections." Adam didn't mind speaking for Bronc. The ranch foreman had a heart of gold, especially when it came to animals. He wouldn't mind checking up on a dog if it brought Prudence peace of mind. "In fact, I'll text him right now."

He did. The response came almost immediately.

On it. No trouble at all.

Adam showed Prudence the message, hoping the concern lines creasing her forehead would ease up. They did as she rattled off the location of the key. Adam sent the information to Bronc, who 'liked' the message.

"I shouldn't stay very long," she said. "I'm needed at the Fritzes'."

"Someone wrote my name down and tucked it inside the blanket, so I'd say you are exactly where you're supposed to be right now," he countered. The fizzle of hope died out the minute she frowned.

3

"Tell me something about you that I don't already know." Adam stared at Prudence. His gaze dipped to her lips and an emotion she wasn't quite prepared to identify passed behind his piercing pale blue eyes.

"I was in the same grade as one of your brothers," she said, clearing her throat to ease the sudden dryness.

"Which one?" he asked.

"Fallon," she supplied.

"That explains why I don't recognize you," he said like her answer satisfied one of the great questions of the universe. "He's six years younger than I am."

"I've walked right past you in the streets." She tried to hide the hurt in her voice.

"I must have been preoccupied," he said.

"You don't have to do that," she said.

He stared at her like she was speaking Greek.

"Pretend like you should have noticed me." She had no idea where that statement came from, but it sure felt good to get it off her chest. Countless folks walked right by her on the rare occasions she was in town without so much as a courtesy nod. As much as she didn't want or need to be the center of attention, her life could be lonely when she was in between jobs. She'd considered getting a dog for company, but she had to be away from home too much looking after other people's pets. It wouldn't be fair to an animal.

"Believe me when I say that I'm not trying to offend you." His chest puffed out a little bit and his back straightened. She had no idea if he even realized he was doing it. But when he crossed his arms over his chest, effectively blocking out anything and everything, she realized she'd put him in a defensive mood.

Since she was here and the baby in her arms needed as many allies as possible, Prudence added, "I wasn't saying that just about you. Most people walk right past without saying a word. I usually prefer not to be noticed." The thought of all those eyes on her sent a shiver racing down her back and made it difficult to breathe.

Relax. Breathe. Repeat. Her mantra had gotten her through some packed rooms and tight spaces without losing her mind. Why did she suddenly *want* to be noticed?

Adam started to open his mouth to speak but then seemed to think better of it. "Do you live in town?"

"Yes," she answered.

"Alone?" He glanced at her wedding ring finger.

"Yes." She held it up to make it easier for him to see there was no diamond, no band, and no tan line. Part of her wondered where her new bravado was coming from. The old Prudence would have withered under Adam's attention. This Prudence sat with her back a little straighter and held her chin up a little higher.

"Boyfriend? Roommate?" he continued.

"Neither. And, no, this angel doesn't belong to me." She

had to admit the baby felt better in her arms than she expected. Natural? That might be pushing it.

"You said you own a pet-sitting business. Right?" he asked.

"Yes. Some folks don't want to bother their neighbors, or they need full-time care for their animals. I mostly work with dogs, but I do have a few cat clients. Henry is an old-timer and he enjoys having company around. We leave the TV on for him set to Animal Planet, not that he's spoiled or anything. But I do cook him fresh meat at night since he has a sensitive stomach." And that was the most words she'd said to any one person outside of necessity or work in longer than she could remember. Had she gotten too comfortable in her own company?

"Do your folks live in town?" he asked.

She shook her head but decided not to elaborate.

"Siblings?" he continued, unfazed by the fact she'd gone quiet.

"When will the sheriff be here?" She checked the clock as her stomach reminded her dinner time was long past. It was dark outside and getting late.

"Soon, I imagine. Although, I don't have to tell you getting in and out of Firebrand Ranch is never a quick endeavor," he said.

"This is my first time to be here, so…" Prudence decided to stop right there before she came across as pitying herself. Not being involved in extracurriculars had been her choice back in school. Reading had always been her favorite thing to do and she'd spent plenty of summers with her nose firmly planted in a book. So much so, the high school English teacher took note and tagged Prudence as an office aid, which worked perfectly for someone who didn't like to sit in boring study hall anyway.

While Prudence jotted down random thoughts from time to time, she never seriously considered trying to write a book despite the occasional pull. Her journal was another story. Whereas some folks had a cell phone glued to their hands, Prudence had her leather-bound notebook as a constant companion.

Speaking of which, it wasn't like her to leave the house without it. She made a mental note to find her purse first thing once the baby's parents were located. And on that note, she asked, "I wonder why the sheriff said no children were reported missing."

"Doesn't mean she wasn't brought across state lines or not reported for some reason or another," he said, catching onto the implication.

"What if her family is out there, somewhere in a ditch or worse?" She couldn't help but wonder. Her mind had a habit of snapping to the worse possible scenario.

"A baby her age wouldn't exactly be able to unstrap herself from a car seat and walk through the woods on her own," he reasoned. "There is probably a logical explanation."

"I just wish I could remember how I found her," she said, drawing a blank on the entire day. "I don't even remember going to check on Henry, but that has to be the reason I'm here."

"About that...does your head hurt when you move it?" A look of concern darkened his otherwise perfect features. He had the kind of sturdy chin and chiseled jawline that ladies drooled over in magazines.

"No." Prudence glanced at his ring finger, confirming what she already knew. He was single.

She redirected her gaze to the baby. More than a smidge of satisfaction filled her that the bundle in her arms was soundly, sweetly sleeping. Content. When was the last time Prudence had felt the same way?

Too long, a little voice in the back of her mind pointed out.

Adam's phone buzzed. He grabbed it and checked the screen. Her stomach picked that moment to growl louder than a hungry bear's. She picked up the glass of water and downed its contents as embarrassment heated her cheeks.

"Sheriff Lawler is out front." He made eye contact like he was looking for approval.

She nodded and smiled before he disappeared down the hallway.

When he returned, a man nearly as tall as Adam, who she recognized as the sheriff, entered the expansive kitchen. Height was where the similarities ended. Lawler was about as fair-skinned as they came, with ginger hair in a military cut. He had a hawk-like nose and compassionate honey-brown eyes along with a smattering of freckles across his face. He wore jeans, boots, and a tan shirt with the word *Sheriff* embroidered on the right front pocket.

"Ms. Owens," Lawler said.

"Please, call me Prudence," she said with that new boldness she felt.

"Okay, Prudence. How are you feeling?" He gave her a once-over like he was checking for blood stains or injuries.

"I'm not hurting anywhere," she confessed.

"Can you tell me everything that happened in your own words?" Lawler asked as Adam motioned toward a chair on the opposite side of the table.

"While you two go over her story, I'm going to heat up dinner," Adam said.

Prudence's stomach groaned and she gave an awkward

smile before turning to the sheriff, who'd taken a seat. "I'm afraid it won't take long to tell you my side of the story."

"Oh?" Lawler said.

"Like Adam said on the phone, I don't remember much of what happened today. All I know is that I have this sweet baby and no idea where she came from or why I have her," she admitted. "I have a dog-sitting job for the Fritzes while they're on vacation. You know Henry, right?"

"He's a sweetheart," he agreed with a quick nod and a concerned look.

"I don't remember anything but that I'm supposed to be looking after him," Prudence said, her shoulders deflating. She couldn't get over the fact it didn't seem like anyone had reported the baby missing. "I was hoping you could tell us who this girl belongs to."

"Tell him about the note," Adam said from across the room. Whatever he was heating up smelled amazing. Or, maybe she was just that hungry. Either way, the minute she handed over the kiddo to her parents, Prudence was going to find something to eat. At this point, she'd take just about anything for how starved she was.

"I found a piece of paper with a name on it," she glanced over at the island where they'd left the slip. "Adam Firebrand."

Lawler cocked an eyebrow at the revelation.

"Do you have any idea why that would happen?" Lawler asked Adam.

He shook his head. "I haven't been in a relationship in a long time and the last one ended with me on one knee and a door in my face."

He'd pretty much sworn off relationships at that point. He was thirty-eight years old and single. And the woman he wanted to spend the rest of his life with had walked out easier than buttering toast. There was about as much fanfare, as well. No returned calls. Yes, he'd gone there. He'd gone down the path of needing a better explanation than the one she gave. *I just don't feel the same way anymore.*

He'd left more texts than he cared to admit while nursing a broken heart. She'd made it clear. She was done. He should accept the fact. Did he, though? No.

He'd wallowed in his misery for months until he woke one morning clear as a bell. No more relationships, only great sex. Again, that annoying voice reminded him that he needed to get started on that. Truth be known, it had held little appeal. He could no longer find the motivation to have sex for the sake of it. He needed something more than physical chemistry, which he strangely felt more of with the woman in his kitchen than he cared to admit.

She had beautiful cobalt blue eyes behind those glasses. They were the kind of blue that was like looking into the depths of the lake, his favorite place.

"Sorry to dredge up the past," Lawler started as Adam pulled out a plate of the best-tasting sour cream chicken enchiladas from the microwave.

Adam grabbed a fork and a paper towel before walking over to the table and placing the meal in front of Prudence. "Do you like enchiladas?"

"I love them and these smell amazing." The way she said the word, *love*, stirred something deep in his chest. He convinced himself it was nothing but a bad memory despite how good it felt.

"Be my guest." He set the fork on the paper towel.

"Thank you," she said. The small smile that lifted up the

corners of full lips caused a chain reaction inside him, spreading warmth through him.

Ignoring it, he heated up a plate for himself after checking with Lawler to make sure he'd eaten. Most folks had. It was getting late. Work started on the ranch at five a.m. Adam was up at four to eat and have time to kick his brain into gear with a few pushups and a large cup of black coffee.

"Don't worry about it," Adam said, picking up on Lawler's conversation thread. "I'm over it all now. It was almost a year ago."

"Excuse the question, but have you had 'relations' with anyone since?" Lawler asked.

Adam wanted to be able to say yes, if only to prove he was over his ex. He shook his head. "Libby was the last...and you already know how that ended."

"So, there's no possibility the child could be yours," Lawler confirmed. "But what about one of your brothers or cousins?"

"None that I've heard of, but we haven't been in the same room and in some cases the same state for months." Adam needed to reach out to everyone to check on the possibility, though.

Lawler turned toward Prudence. "I put out a call to see if any neighboring communities have reported a missing child."

"It's strange, isn't it?" Prudence's forehead scrunched up. She'd already made quick work of the enchiladas. "That no one has come forward to say their baby is missing."

"I would agree," Lawler confirmed. "There has to be extenuating circumstances."

"Like what?" she pressed.

"The parents might not realize she's missing. They could

be away or working. Something might have happened while she was in the care of a sitter," he said.

"Wouldn't *someone* notice a baby? She's too little to take care of herself." The answer seemed to dawn on Prudence when she sucked in a burst of air. "She might have been kidnapped."

Lawler nodded.

"Then, doesn't that make me the number one suspect?" she asked.

"Normally, I'd say yes. Except you're here with Adam, calling the law to find out what happened. I'm concerned you were struck and that's why your memory is being blocked," he said. "Trauma can cause temporary memory loss."

"I'm willing to cooperate in any way that I can. But I have to take care of Henry in the meantime," she said.

Adam caught the look Lawler gave hearing her response.

"My family is well known in the area," Adam said, redirecting the conversation, figuring he needed to ask Lawler what that was about in private. "It might be the reason for the note. Maybe someone decided she would be safer in the protection of a Firebrand."

"I'd say that's a good theory. One I plan to investigate." Lawler was holding back. Did he suspect Prudence was playing some kind of twisted game?

For reasons Adam couldn't explain, he didn't like suspicion being cast on her. Along those same lines, his protective instincts flared, and he wanted to protect her despite the fact she'd proven fully capable of helping herself. He surprised himself in the fact he wanted to know more about her. She'd closed up when he asked about her parents. Why? She changed the subject when he'd asked about siblings. Again, why?

"I have someone coming to take care of Baby X while we get to the bottom of what happened and return her to her family." Lawler spoke with compassion.

Prudence frowned and Adam could've sworn she tightened her arms around the baby. She had a look on her face he imagined a mother bear might have if someone tried to mess with one of her cubs.

"Like who?" Adam asked, not liking the idea of 'Baby X' being carted off by a stranger.

"A representative from child services," Lawler said. He wasn't giving away much. Didn't he trust Prudence?

"What will happen to the baby during the investigation?" Adam continued.

"She'll be placed in foster care," Lawler supplied in a sympathetic voice.

"Someone wanted her brought to me." Adam didn't like the idea of the little girl being bounced around.

His cell buzzed. He checked the screen. There was a call coming in from Bronc.

Adam walked over to the sink and answered.

"How's Henry?" he immediately asked his foreman.

"Fine, boss. The Fritzes got back three days ago," Bronc said, not able to hide the shock in his voice.

Adam bit back a curse. Was that the reason Lawler kept looking at her strangely when she brought up her client?

4

———

The look on Adam's face caused a fireball to swirl in the pit of Prudence's stomach. He thanked Bronc for information before ending the call and turning to face her. He didn't have to open his mouth for her to realize bad news was coming.

She took a drink of water, trying to douse the hot bile rising in the back of her throat as she waited for news that something bad had happened to the Fritz couple.

"First of all, Henry is fine," he said to her. "But your job ended with the Fritzes three days ago."

"What?" She shook her head, her body stiffened, and the baby stirred. Not wanting to disturb the angel's sleep, Prudence forced calm she didn't feel. "How can that be? I was there earlier today. I'm supposed to..."

Realization struck out of nowhere like lightning on a cloudless sky. Prudence balanced the baby against her body with one arm, holding her close, while bringing the other one up to check for bumps on her own head.

"What's your full name?" Lawler asked. Leaning forward.

"Prudence Abigail Owens," she supplied, figuring cooperation would bring closure to this nightmare sooner rather than later.

"Date of birth?" he asked.

She rattled it off. "I don't have any ID on me. If you want proof, you'll have to give me a ride to my house."

She hoped her purse was there. How could she have lost three days?

"What day of the week is it?" Lawler continued.

"Sunday," she blew out a sigh. "That can't be right. It has to be Wednesday because the Fritzes got back from vacation over the weekend."

At least Henry was fine, and she hadn't neglected him. She shouldn't have another sitting job for a week and a half, so she was good there. The thought of letting any of her customers down when they needed her struck like a physical blow. She hadn't, she reminded herself. So far, so good.

Adam stared at the tile flooring. She wished he'd say something or look at her. It was strange how much she wanted to see his reaction.

"Do you know what month it is?" Lawler didn't miss a beat.

She took a second to calculate. "That would make it June."

Lawler nodded and gave a reassuring look. "You're doing fine."

She didn't feel it. This didn't seem like a good time to point out the fact.

The doorbell rang and she froze.

"Excuse me. I'll be right back," Adam said to them both. His eyes still seemed unable to meet hers.

True to his word, Adam returned a few moments later with a woman in her late thirties to early forties trailing behind him. Her blonde hair was tied back in a ponytail. Her face fresh, her heels high, she had on a dark suit.

All Prudence could think was that this stranger was not walking out the door with the baby.

The dark suit walked straight over to Sheriff Lawler. The two shook hands and Lawler asked her if she'd like to take a seat. She declined, instead keeping a distance and leaning a hip against the large granite island anchoring the room. Adam reclaimed the spot where he'd been standing, and Prudence's neck hairs bristled at how close the two of them stood. Not that where Adam Firebrand stood was any of her business.

Except a little voice in the back of her mind argued he was somehow connected to the child in her arms—a child she had no plans to abandon.

"Is it possible the birth mother got into trouble? Changed her mind about being fit to take care of a baby? Left her on a doorstep with the note?" Prudence asked after being introduced to Dark Suit, whose actual name was Jenn Pratt.

"It's too early to rule anything out," Lawler said.

She appreciated him for not stating the obvious, that she could be the one who took the baby from someone. Again, she went back to the fact there would be someone out there searching for the sweet little girl.

"I apologize for asking the question, but have you had any alcoholic beverages today?" Lawler asked.

Adam blew out a sharp breath and pinched the bridge of his nose.

"No. At least, I don't think so," she admitted. There was no way to be certain if she couldn't remember how or when she'd come up with a baby.

"Do you have a habit of taking illegal substances?" Lawler continued.

Adam muttered a curse before dropping his hand. "Come on."

"I have to ask tough questions, Adam. I wouldn't be doing my job otherwise." His explanation didn't calm Adam down. Although, he did nod his understanding.

"No. I don't take drugs, illegal or otherwise. I'd be happy to show you my medicine cabinet at home where you'll find vitamins and medication prescribed specifically to me," she defended.

The room sat quiet for too long. The silence made Prudence uncomfortable.

Then, Lawler leaned forward, placing his elbows on his knees. "Jenn is here to take the baby and I need your full cooperation for a smooth transition."

"Does she have to? Can't she interview me? I'll volunteer to care for the baby until you find her next of kin or what about..." Hope died on Prudence's lips as she spoke. She didn't finish her sentence before the sheriff was shaking his head.

"I'm sorry," was all he said.

"Hear me out," she continued. "She knows me, and we have formula for her. Casey brought up diapers and wipes. There's plenty to get through the night. Plus, she's already asleep and—"

"That's impossible," Lawler cut her off. He didn't seem like he was trying to be rude. In fact, he seemed more like he was trying to stop a roaring train before it slammed into a wall. He waved his hands in the air. "Jenn here is trained in how to handle these delicate situations. She'll find an appropriate temporary home—"

"She deserves to stay where she's comfortable," Prudence whispered. "And that seems to be here with me."

"Like I said, ma'am, I apologize for being unable to grant your request. You're welcome to fill out an application to become a foster parent—"

"That could take weeks or months to set up. It would be too late," Adam intervened. He'd been standing off to the side, watching quietly as the whole scene unfolded. When he finally looked up, he had fire in his eyes.

A trill of excitement that he would take up for her rocketed through her, fueling her. "What if I hand over access to my accounts? Let you come check my medicine cabinet to make sure I'm not taking anything that could hamper my ability to care for her?"

Again, Lawler shook his head.

"What are we talking about here?" Adam added. "An overnight stay?"

"Yes. Overnight to start," Lawler said. "We don't know the circumstances yet, though. This could end up dragging on for days, possibly weeks."

"I'm willing to go the distance until she's safe in her own bed again," Prudence volunteered. She understood the pickle he was in. How could he give a baby to someone who couldn't remember how she came across her in the first place?

"There's no need to do that," Adam said with the kind of finality that would put him in the head seat in any board room. "How about this. She stays here with me. I take care of her."

"You sure you want to do that with everything you have going on?" Lawler asked.

"My name was tucked inside the blanket, Timothy. I've never been more certain of anything in my life." Adam turned to Jenn. "Thank you for stopping by. It doesn't look like we'll be needing your services after all."

ADAM'S MIND was made up. Someone had written his name on a slip of paper. Prudence was on his family's property and she'd been one hundred percent honest about everything she remembered. He could see it in her eyes. Plus, there was no reason for her to lie.

"Sheriff?" Jenn's gaze bounced from him to Lawler and back.

Lawler gave a nod.

"Mind if I check her out before I leave? For my report," Jenn said.

"Be my guest," Adam said, figuring Jenn would have to examine Baby X while in Prudence's arms. There was something about the look of determination in her eyes that had forced him to do the right thing. Plus, he was more than a little curious as to why his name had come up.

It was late and, based on the fact Prudence had yawned no less than three times in the past five minutes, he figured she could use a good night of sleep. Everything would look better in the morning and they could figure out a plan from there. By then, the parents of this sleeping angel might have come forward and the reunion would be sweet.

Wishful thinking?

He needed something positive to happen in his life considering he was still reeling from the Marshall's death and the aftermath that was as certain as a tornado in April.

Prudence opened the blanket enough for Jenn to count ten fingers and ten toes. She noted a birthmark behind the baby's right ear.

"How old would you guess she is?" Prudence whispered.

"A couple of weeks, five at the most," Jenn said.

"Someone must be frantic, or they will be when they realize she's missing." Prudence's sympathy and protective stance was the main reason he'd volunteered to keep the baby overnight.

Maybe it was losing the Marshall that had Adam's heart feeling tender. He didn't normally do knee-jerk reactions. All he could do was stand by the fact it seemed like the right thing to do.

Besides, he was more than mildly confused as to why his name came up in connection with this case. His curiosity about Prudence was growing. If she truly didn't have family around, he figured no one had her back.

"I'll file a report and make sure the information about her being located is on the database as soon as possible," Lawler said. He grabbed his phone and asked if he could snap a picture for the file.

Prudence nodded.

"She looks perfect to me," Jenn said with a cautious smile. She didn't seem thrilled about the arrangement but didn't look ready to go up against the sheriff either.

"I promise to take good care of her until her family is located," Prudence reassured.

"I have no doubt you will." Jenn's words were appreciated. She turned to the sheriff. "If that's all, I'd like to get back to my own family."

"Thank you for coming out on short notice," Lawler said. He stood up and walked her out of the room, no doubt to convince her that he was doing the right thing for the baby. He would want her endorsement on an important matter like this one.

As the pair disappeared down the hallway, Prudence wasted no time thanking him.

"I do understand why I'm not exactly a good candidate to take care of her by myself. This wouldn't be happening without your help," she said to Adam.

He wasn't ready to make a big deal out of it, but his chest filled with pride that he'd made her happy.

"What do we need to do to get the two of you to bed?" He immediately heard the way that sounded and backtracked. "That didn't—"

"I think I know what you meant," she said, and her cheeks turned a couple shades of pink. The coloring contrasted against her creamy skin and brought out those intensely beautiful eyes.

"Shower? Clothes? More food? Something to drink? Name it and it's yours," he said, redirecting his thoughts.

"Part of me doesn't want to risk waking her. She looks so peaceful. Finally," she added on a sigh.

"We know her lungs are in full working order," he joked, needing to lighten the mood.

Prudence had an incredible smile when she relaxed. Thick, full lips that curled at the corners that he suddenly wanted to kiss.

Since that would be about as productive as milking a flower, he steered his thoughts in a different direction.

"We can stay here overnight or head over to my place," he said.

"You don't live here?" she asked, glancing around.

"This house belongs...*belonged*...to my grandfather," he stated.

"I'm sorry, Adam. I heard the sheriff reference your family but I didn't realize anything serious had happened."

Her voice was like silk, trailing over him, soothing places he kept hidden.

"Yesterday," he said by way of explanation.

"Makes sense I don't know, considering I have no memories of the past three days," she said low and under her breath. "I wonder what else I've been missing."

"Not much. You were right about it being June. Even if you did take a blow to the head, you're speaking clearly. You seem to have your wits about you now," he said.

"What about the ER?" she asked.

"Do you feel queasy?" He'd grown up with eight brothers and nine cousins. He knew a thing or two about concussions.

"No," she said.

"Is your sight blurry?" he continued.

"Only when I take off my glasses." She did, and he was struck by her high cheekbones and silky skin. Her eyes stood out even more, if that was possible, framed by thick lashes. And those lips rounded an oval-shaped face that caused his heart to skip a few beats when he stared at it too long.

How had he walked right past her and never noticed?

Crazy how much he'd missed by keeping his head down and never looking around. To be fair, he knew just about everyone in town and usually kept his eyes forward rather than risk long conversations with people. Adam almost laughed out loud at the thought. If he didn't know any better, he'd call himself an introvert.

Give him a clear day, an endless sky, decent weather, and not another human for miles. That sounded like perfection until now. He'd never thought of his life as lonely before. Not even in the past ten months when he'd been licking his wounds. What was the sudden difference?

Losing the Marshall was playing with Adam's head. Or was it something else? Because suddenly, looking at Prudence holding that baby in her arms, it seemed like there was more to life that he'd been missing by keeping his eyes on the ground.

The sound of Lawler's boots shuffling across the tile in the hallway interrupted the moment.

"Jenn is all set," Lawler said.

"How about you?" Adam walked over and placed his hand on Lawler's shoulder. "Are you good with this arrangement?"

"I better be. I just sent my only social worker home." Lawler laughed at his own joke. "Seriously, Baby X is lucky to stay here on the ranch. I couldn't find a better overnight situation for her if I tried. I have complete faith the two of you will take excellent care of her."

Prudence's face lit up at the compliment, and it warmed Adam's heart. He'd just volunteered to keep a newborn overnight along with letting a stranger with no memory of the past three days stay in the Marshall's home. Maybe Adam was the one who'd lost his mind.

5

P rudence rocked the baby. Her arms were ready to fall off. Her back hurt. And, strangely, she'd never felt better in her life.

Unless, of course, she factored in the reality she had no memory whatsoever of the last three days.

"I know the way out," Lawler said after asking a few more routine-sounding questions for his report. The man had been thorough.

He disappeared down the hallway as Adam caught her gaze.

"For tonight, it's probably best if we stay here. There haven't been any kids in this place in years and we'll have privacy since I doubt anyone will want to stay at the Marshall's house. Anyone who wanted one has a home on the property," Adam said. "And I know a bedroom with a crib already set up. I don't think the room has been used since my brothers were little."

"Why is there two of everything?" Prudence asked, remembering her question from earlier. At least her mind was working now.

Adam stopped cold. His forehead wrinkled in confusion.

"When Luna brought us here. I noticed two sets of barns and—"

"Oh, right." Adam nodded. "It's because my father and uncle fight so much. Have all their lives. So, the Marshall built two separate but equal homes and barns for them. The whole place is divided down the middle."

The dread in his voice struck her.

"It sounds like a rough situation to grow up in," she said. Looking around at all the grandeur, she'd assumed living here must be a dream. The family had plenty of money. At least, that's how it looked from the outside.

"Believe me, you don't want to know." He issued a sharp sigh before holding out his hand. "How about we talk about that later? I'm not sure how long one of those things sleeps, but Casey comes back from his weekends at home more tired than if he'd spent all day on fences."

"Fences?" She quirked a brow, noticing he'd just called Baby X a 'thing.' She was mildly amused by the off-handed comment.

"Remind me to explain what that means another time," he said with a smile and a wink.

She took his outstretched hand and used it as leverage to pull herself up. There was something about making contact with Adam that caused electricity to vibrate through her, warming her all the way to her cheekbones and back.

"Think we can head to my place first thing in the morning? I have a prescription there and can't miss a dose," she said.

"Not a problem. I have a feeling Baby—"

"Mind if we figure out a nickname for her? I hate the thought of referring to her in such a generic term," Prudence said.

"Let's see. I was standing on Angel Pass when I first—"

"Angel. I like that name," she said with a smile. "What do you think?"

"It's good. It fits her." He looked at the baby in her arms with such appreciation that Prudence's ovaries practically hummed.

"Let's put Angel to bed and give your arms a break," he said.

"Deal."

Prudence followed him upstairs and to the first bedroom on the right. The room was large. It had a four-poster bed, wallpaper that was elegant but also from a different era, and a sitting area complete with a balcony.

"I picked this suite for its size, the en suite bath, and the fact that, if memory serves, there's a crib on the other side of the bed," he said.

"If you don't come up here, why is it so clean?" She didn't see a speck of dust.

"The Marshall had a live-in housekeeper for years. She'll be back tomorrow morning. It was next to impossible to force her to take the night off and go home," he said.

"I thought you said she lived here," she said.

"Only during the weekdays," he stated.

True to his word, there was an old-fashioned crib next to the bed. Prudence glanced at the clock, realizing she didn't so much as have her phone on her. It was strange to be so disconnected, but she missed her journal even more. She almost laughed out loud. What exactly would she write in it? Forgot the past three days but woke up with a baby and none other than Adam Firebrand at my side.

If only it was funny.

Prudence glanced down at her clothes. She must have been around some animal today considering the dog hair on her jogging suit. Please don't tell her she'd been wearing the same clothes for three days. She shook off the thought as impossible. She would smell much worse.

Although, would she even know it if she did?

Embarrassment heated her cheeks at the thought. There would have been a sign if she stunk to high heaven. Right? A wrinkled nose when Adam got close to her.

She decided she must not be too ripe. A shower still sounded amazing and she wondered if there was any clothing she could borrow in the meantime.

"Do you, by chance, have something I can change into after a shower? I always take one before bed and these clothes are dirty." She had to wash off the animal funk before climbing under her sheets.

"There's a robe on the back of the door. That should do until I can throw your clothes in the washer." His voice dropped an octave and had a low-gravelly quality to it that caused her stomach to freefall.

"That's great." She cleared her throat trying to ease the sudden dryness. Why did it feel like she'd just licked a glue stick? Prudence gently placed the baby in the crib. "Think she'll be okay here until I get back?"

"I'll make sure of it." Those words spoken with that voice traveled all over her.

Prudence had no choice but to get out of Dodge. She practically gaited toward the bathroom.

"Toss your clothes out and I'll run them through while you shower," he said. That man could make reading the ingredients off a cereal box sound sexy.

"Okay." The thought of him touching her most personal things sent more of that electricity shooting through her. She stripped and then wrapped a towel around her. Even the towels here were bigger and better than anything she'd ever owned.

Cracking the door open, she handed over her clothes, bra, and panties in all. She'd been careful to tuck those inside her warm-up shirt, but still. *Shower.*

For the next ten minutes, she scrubbed and rinsed. Did Angel need to be cleaned up too? Prudence somehow doubted the baby took a daily bath. If she had her phone, she could easily look it up. She'd learned a long time ago that she could figure out how to do almost anything within reason on the internet.

The sounds of Angel fussing got Prudence moving. She exited the shower, dried off, and wrapped the robe around her in two shakes.

Nothing could prepare her for the hit she took when she opened the door and saw this huge, outdoorsy cattle rancher trying to calm the baby. Angel looked so tiny by comparison to his big strong arms. He was gently bouncing her on his shoulder while comforting her by patting her back.

The sight was almost too much to take in all at once. A surprising tear sprang to her eye. Prudence had never once wanted a husband and a child. Not as far back as she could remember had either of those things held any appeal. Until this moment. Right then. With Adam and Angel.

ADAM HAD HELPED with kittens and foals, and had assisted with the birthing of puppies and more calves than he could count, so why was this little thing ripping his heart to shreds with her whimper?

He'd never felt so helpless in all his life.

"Everything okay in here?" Prudence's voice was like rain in a drought.

"She's fussy so I picked her up. It helped for all of two seconds," he said, trying not to notice the rivulet of water rolling down Prudence's sensual neck. She didn't have her glasses on, so he could see more of the delicate features of her face. *Not the time, Firebrand.*

"I can take her," she offered but he figured her arms needed a break.

"Tell me what to do and I'll do it," he said.

"She can't be hungry again so soon..." A spark lit up her dark blue eyes as she wagged her finger in the air and headed toward the loveseat where he'd set the diaper bag. She returned a moment later with something blue in her hand.

"There you go." She barely touched Angel's cheek with it before the newborn latched on.

It was insta-quiet.

"What is that thing?" he asked.

"A pacifier," she said with a smile that spread warmth through his chest—a chest that had been encased in ice for the past year.

He walked over to the crib and gently placed her back inside. "Is there a right way to do this?"

"I think she has to be on her back," she said.

There was something satisfying about getting the baby to settle down and rest. He had a feeling they were in for a ride tonight, though. When Prudence moved next to him, his racing heart agreed.

Rather than allow that train to pick up steam, he excused himself to take a shower. "Will you be okay alone with her?"

A look of hurt passed behind her eyes.

"I don't mean you're incapable or that you'll hurt her in any way," he quickly back-peddled. "I wanted to make sure you were comfortable with it."

"You were," she said and he could hear the defensiveness in her tone.

"I had you in the next room. My clothes are in a different wing." This place had always felt too big for so few people living here. Unlike his sons, the Marshall only had two children. This place was more than half empty all of the time. It seemed like a waste of space to Adam, who preferred his two-bedroom log cabin by the lake. Azure Lake had always been his favorite spot on the ranch when he needed to get away from it all and think.

Her mouth formed the word, oh.

"In that case, how long will it take you to get back?" she asked.

"Depends on your comfort level. I can jog to the other side of the house and back, or shower over there where all my stuff is. Your choice," he said.

"You should go where you're comfortable," she stated. "I'll be fine here."

He paused for a second as his brain started clicking.

"You know what's strange to me?" he asked.

She shook her head.

"I've been talking to you for..." He glanced at the clock on the nightstand. It was almost midnight. "Three hours now and you haven't slipped once. You know your name. You know what day it is. Your mind is sharp."

"I thought the same thing in the shower," she admitted on a heavy sigh. "It's weird, isn't it."

"What's the last thing you remember?" he asked.

"Waking up," she said. "The next part isn't so clear, but it involves Henry."

That was three days ago. "And you have no memories since then?"

"That's right," she said.

"No one stopped by to see him and you didn't go anywhere else?" he asked.

"Not that I remember," she admitted with a shrug. "Frustrating, isn't it."

"It's a puzzle for me. I can only imagine what a terrible feeling it must be for you," he said. There had to be something...an event? His mind snapped to her being on a date and someone slipping something inside her drink.

Her mind was sharp now. She seemed to be firing on all cylinders.

"We'll get to the bottom of what's going on," he said as he headed toward the hallway.

"I'm not sure if I thanked you nearly enough, Adam." The sound of her voice stopped him in his tracks. The mix of gratitude tinted with fear the memory lapse could strike at any time strengthened his resolve.

"No need. It's what we do here. We take care of our own," he said and meant it. Ranchers were known for having each other's backs. He couldn't exactly speak for folks in town, but that spirit was very much alive and well when it came to his community.

"I appreciate it anyway. You didn't have to stick up for me with Lawler or volunteer to let me and Angel stay here overnight. It means a lot that you would put yourself out for me, for her," she said. Her voice cracked on the last part and he wondered if her emotions were getting the best of her. He couldn't imagine how awful it would be to lose three days of his life, just like that with no warning.

She didn't appear sick or hurt. She was too young for dementia. It just didn't add up.

"You're welcome, Prudence," he said. "This all must be crazy for you. My guess is that you acted quickly to save that little girl's life. You saw the piece of paper, my name, and were bringing her here to the ranch when something else happened. I can only imagine why you would be on that part of the land, but every possibility causes my hands to fist and anger to well up. Helping you fill in the details is the least I can do."

"Is that really what you think?" She was reaching for hope. He could hear it in her voice. She needed a reason not to be scared to go to sleep or wake up in the morning.

"I wouldn't say so if it wasn't true. Hand to God," he said.

She sat on the edge of the bed and took a deep breath. "So, we'll figure it out together?"

"You have my word," he said.

His answer seemed to satisfy her. At least for the time being. She seemed nervous about turning in.

"I'll be back in a few minutes. Fifteen tops." He figured he could make it to the opposite wing and scrub down in roughly that amount of time.

"Then, I'll wait up for you," she offered, fiddling with the belt on her robe. Nervous habit?

He glanced at the bed. It hadn't occurred to him they'd be sleeping in the same room. Now that he thought about it, it made sense. She would probably want the company and she seemed more than a little afraid to wake up, like sleeping might somehow erase her memories again.

The way she looked at him right then would haunt him if that happened. He tried not to let that dominate his thoughts as he cut across the house to the other wing.

6

Prudence exhaled the minute Adam returned. It felt like she'd been holding her breath for the past seventeen minutes. Impossible, she knew. But that was what it felt like when her lifeline walked out of the room.

Until she figured out what was happening with her memory, she planned to stick to him like red on velvet. She hoped the move wouldn't be too annoying or last too long. Then again, being with Adam wasn't the hard part. Missing entire days from her life was scary.

What else had she done or seen that she was possibly suppressing? Was there some trauma behind her current situation with Angel? It made sense there would be. Then there was Prudence's anxiety. Normally, it was through the roof in unknown situations and places. Sleeping over at a stranger's house should have her clamoring for the front door. Instead, she felt like she'd come home. Though that feeling was dependent on Adam being in the room. Was she attached to him because he'd been her savior today? A knight in shining armor, so to speak. Except said knight was one gorgeous, honorable, and strong cowboy?

Who wouldn't feel a draw to someone like that?

"When do you think she needs her next bottle?" Adam asked, taking a seat on the bed in between her and the baby. The mattress dipped under his weight.

"Good question," she said. "I'm thinking she'll let us know."

"And loudly, at that," he said with a smirk.

Prudence laughed. She could watch that kid sleep for hours. But she needed to rest while she could. *If* she could. And that was a big *if.* The very real fear the day would be erased when she woke up the next morning caused an icy chill to race down her back, gripping her spine. An uneasy feeling settled over her, like a dark cloud engulfing her.

"She's a little bit of perfection," she said. "I know someone out there must be missing her hard. No matter what the situation ends up being."

"I can't imagine how horrible it must be to give up or lose a child," he said. "Not that I ever planned on having any of my own."

"Really?" she asked before she could rein it in. His position on having a family wasn't her business, and yet he'd said it so casually like it was set in stone.

"Why does that surprise you?" He cocked a dark brow, and she didn't want to focus on how sexy it was, *he* was. The nightlight hit his face just right, highlighting his strong jaw. But then, there probably wasn't any lighting that could make him look bad.

"I don't know," she stammered. "You come from a big family and grew up here on the ranch. This place is impressive to say the least. You are obviously close with Brax. I noticed that right away when I met him earlier. I just assumed all this would come with having a big family of your own someday."

"Yeah?" He seemed genuinely caught off guard at her response. "None of *this* guarantees a happy life. Not the big house. The Marshall lived here, and I guarantee you that man wasn't content a day in his life. He wasn't close with either of his sons and now his death promises to divide the family further." He stopped himself like he'd caught himself in an intense moment, and then a casual smile broke out on his near-perfect face. "But, hey, you didn't come here for all that."

Prudence realized she'd overstepped her bounds. An apology didn't seem fitting. Besides, she'd done that twice already. She actually wanted to know more about Adam, but he'd erected a wall the minute he realized he was sharing from deep down.

"Isn't it funny how easy it is to make snap judgments about someone's life?" she said. "It's unfair."

"Half the reason I'm alive today is relying on gut instinct. We aren't usually wrong," he reasoned, and his tone was much more thoughtful now. All the defensiveness was gone.

"True, which can make it all that much more awful when we are." She bit back a yawn.

"I'm keeping you awake," he pushed off the bed.

"No, you're not." She didn't want him to leave and yet sleeping in the same bed felt a little dangerous if she was being honest. "I hate to admit this...but I'm afraid to go to sleep."

"Because the last thing you remember is waking up?" he asked, but it was more statement than a question.

"Yes." She pulled the covers up.

"I doubt we'll get much more than an hour or two before Angel wakes up," he said. "So, how about this. I promise to remind you of everything that happened today. I'll tell you all the details until they're so etched in your memory that you won't be able to forget them if you tried. How does that sound?"

Like a promise he might not be able to keep.

"Deal." She didn't want to deflate his chest and it really was a beautiful answer. "I just wish I had my journal with me." Add her cell phone, purse, and a few other items to the list. She didn't realize how much she would miss until they were gone. Gone might be a strong word, away from her.

"Goodnight," was the last thing she heard before she nodded off.

It felt like she'd barely closed her eyes when she heard Angel fussing. She reached for her glasses. A quick glance at the clock said it was one o'clock in the morning. So, she'd gotten all of an hour of uninterrupted sleep.

The minute she moved, Adam was by her side. He froze the second they made eye contact.

"I remember," she said, and he seemed to really exhale.

"That's good," he reassured, and it looked like a weight lifted off his shoulders. "I'll run down and make a bottle while you try to soothe her. I watched Casey yesterday, so I should be good."

Adam standing next to the bed with no shirt on and jeans slung low on his hips was the kind of image she could get used to waking up to.

Prudence threw the covers off as he disappeared out the door. He must've fallen asleep on the loveseat because the other side of the bed was still made. There were no wrinkles on the duvet. Seriously, the bed was big enough for both of them to sleep without ever touching each other. She would bring it up when he got back with the bottle.

For now, her full attention was going to Angel.

"Hey, sweet girl," she soothed as she picked her up. She located the binky, which had been spit out at some point in the past hour, and bit back a yawn. "This all must be very confusing for you, but we are going to take good care of you tonight."

This little bean had quickly wormed her way into Prudence's heart. As much as she couldn't wait to reunite Angel with her parents, the moment would be bittersweet.

A laugh tickled her throat at the fact she remembered. She'd been so scared her mind would be a blank slate when she woke. Grateful for the small miracle, she couldn't help but smile. The binky did its job, keeping Angel satisfied long enough for Adam to return with the real deal.

He handed over the bottle, but Prudence had an idea.

"How about you do the honors," she said.

"I don't know about that. She might not want someone else to do it," he reasoned.

"Sit down next to me and give it a try." She had no idea where her bravado was coming from. She wasn't normally this straight-forward. But it was nice.

Adam did as requested. She handed him the baby, and her heart took another hit at the image. She handed over the bottle next and then pulled the binky out of Angel's mouth. He didn't have to score a direct hit. The little girl was already rooting for the nipple. She contentedly sucked away the second she found it.

"We'll need to burp her, and she'll probably need a diaper change after her meal," she said. They were figuring her routine out.

"Looks like we got four hours in between feedings," he noted. "That's an intense schedule if it's twenty-four hours a day."

The image of Adam Firebrand giving a baby a bottle

would stick with her for a very long time. At least, she hoped it would when she woke in the morning.

PRUDENCE'S MEMORY loss was a real head scratcher.

With Angel's feeding schedule, Adam saw that it would be difficult to accomplish much else in a day. He tipped his hat to all the mothers and fathers out there, doing this every day, especially the ones doing this alone. Don't even get him started on folks who had multiple children to look after. They deserved a medal as far as he was concerned.

He fed, burped, and changed the little girl with Prudence's help. Then, he gently placed her back in the crib. Angel was back to doing what babies seemed to do best, namely sleeping in short bursts.

"The loveseat can't possibly be comfortable," Prudence said.

He had a crick in his neck to prove it, but he didn't want her to feel like she was putting him out. "I've slept in worse places."

"The bed is huge. You could sleep on the other side and our body parts wouldn't get anywhere near each other," she said with a boldness that didn't fit the image of a woman who could blend in with the background. She'd insisted they'd passed each other, and he believed her. His main thought now was, *How could he have missed her*?

"It's no trouble," he countered, figuring he didn't need to go there. Even a dirty jogging suit couldn't hide those long legs of hers—legs with creamy skin that his fingers were itching to get lost on. The naked image of her in the shower had been difficult to wipe from his thoughts.

"We can roll up a blanket and put it in the middle," she

volunteered. "Or how about these pillows? They're long enough to block any physical contact."

She was tempting fire and didn't seem to realize it.

The loveseat was uncomfortable, and he would be lucky if Angel gave them another four hours. Plus, Prudence seemed intent on not inconveniencing him.

"I promise not to touch you," she added.

"Shame," he said under his breath as he walked over to his side of the bed.

"Sorry, I didn't catch that," she said.

"It was nothing." He got comfortable and closed his eyes. She seemed content to let it go. Not much got past her. She had a sharp mind, which confused him even more about her memory episode. With no visible head injury to blame, he was drawing a blank on what could be causing it. For a split-second, the thought crossed his mind she could be sick or have some type of brain tumor. He tried not to put too much stock in it. Depending on what happened when she woke in the morning, he would insist she get checked out by a doctor.

First, they needed to find Angel's parents.

Real sleep was impossible, but he drifted around for a while in his thoughts. A growing part of him hoped Prudence woke with all her memories intact, especially yesterday. He'd talked to her more openly about his family than anyone else, including Libby. He chalked it up to the Marshall's death. Adam was being sentimental for once. He supposed loss had a way of doing that to a person. The real surprise came with the fact he wanted to tell her more. She needed sleep, though. He'd seen the dark circles cradling those incredible blue eyes. He didn't want to be the reason she walked around in a fog tomorrow.

In fact, if he could manage, he would wake and feed the

baby before Angel had time to wind up. Prudence would be able to get a solid, much-needed eight hours in.

Adam kept one eye on the clock as he listened to Prudence's steady, even breathing. Her sleep was peaceful, making him drop 'trauma' to the bottom of possibilities for memory loss. There was no way to rule it out completely, but instinct said she would work it out in her dreams, unless she'd suppressed it so far that resurfacing would take weeks, maybe months. Wouldn't there be some sign of struggle if that were the case?

The baby shifted and he slipped out of the covers with stealth-like movement. Without making a sound, he scooped the little girl up. Pride filled his chest for being able to handle her so easily already. The first time she was in his arms, he was afraid he would hurt her. Being wrapped up like a burrito helped. Her arms and legs were tucked in there tight. He grabbed the binky, which seemed to satisfy her for the time being.

Rather than wake Prudence, he shouldered the diaper bag and headed downstairs to the kitchen, unsure how he was going to pull off making a bottle while holding Angel.

The light was on. The smell of coffee wafted down the hallway. Had Miss Olive come back early? She was due today, but four in the morning was a stretch.

His brother Brax's back was to Adam as he entered the room.

"Hey, what are you doing here so early?" Adam asked, thankful for an extra pair of hands.

"Wanted to check in with you before the day took off." Brax turned around.

Out on the land, cell service could be spotty and it was easy to get lost in the work, forgetting all sense of time.

"Mind helping me make a bottle?" Adam could manage

a diaper change. Based on the grunt followed by a rank smell, she needed one.

"Tell me what to do." Brax was the second oldest and the two of them had always been close.

Adam rattled off instructions and Brax had the bottle ready by the time Angel's diaper change was finished. "Do you want to do the honors?"

"Feed her?" Brax wrinkled his nose and shook his head. "I'd rather take that thing outside to the trash."

"It'll sure keep pesky critters out of the bin." Adam laughed. No rummaging around in there with that smell. For something so tiny, she sure could clear out the place. It dawned on him what Casey had said about mixing formula. His son's must not be the one she was used to.

Brax grabbed the folded-up diaper and headed out the back door. He returned a minute later. "What's the story?"

"Best we can tell is that Prudence came into possession of her and was trying to get to me when I found her lost on the property," he said.

"Why you?" Brax's eyebrow shot up.

"That's the question of the day," Adam admitted. "There was a note tucked inside her blanket with a scribble of my name on it."

"Huh." Brax reclaimed his mug and took a sip of coffee.

"Mind pouring a cup for me?" Adam asked. He could use a caffeine boost to clear his head.

Brax did before walking over and setting it down on the table next to where Adam had planted himself. He studied the baby for a long moment. "Any chance she's yours?"

"I haven't been with anyone since Libby and I doubt she is the type to keep something this big from me," he said. "The timing doesn't work because we hadn't..." He glanced up at his brother, figuring there was such a thing as too much information and it was a line he was about to cross. "Anyway, I don't see how it would be possible."

"Have you reached out to her?" Brax's question was logical.

"She didn't return my calls before. Why would that change now?" Adam shook his head.

He examined the little girl's features. So she had black hair. There wasn't much of it. And her eyes were blue, more the color of Prudence's than his. An unfamiliar emotion stirred in his chest when he really looked at her.

"What do you plan to do with her?" Brax asked.

"Nothing," Adam answered a little too quickly. "What I meant to say is, the sheriff will find her parents and we'll get a call any minute now."

"Wouldn't that have happened already?" Brax glanced up at the clock on the wall. "If they were alive."

The reality Adam had been trying to avoid smacked him square in the chest.

"To be honest, I didn't want to consider that as a possibility. She has to have some relative who would want her," he said. It would be a mistake to get too attached to her no matter how adorable she was. This little nugget wouldn't get past his defenses.

"I'm surprised there isn't an all-points bulletin for a missing child. Aren't you?" Brax asked.

Adam nodded, but he needed to change the subject. "What about the Marshall? Any word on the will?"

Brax compressed his lips.

"All I know is that no one is talking, which can't be a good sign," he said.

"Wouldn't our lawyer wait until everyone was in town before giving out details?" Adam had been so consumed with Angel and Prudence that he hadn't given much thought to anything else, including his family's situation. It was only a matter of time before the ticking bomb when off. Him, Brax, and the others would be left to pick up the pieces.

"It's possible," Brax said. "I'm not sure if everyone can or will come home."

Between the military and family feuds, he could name a couple of cousins and a few brothers who'd promised not to darken the door of this building anytime soon. Surely they didn't mean in case of death.

"It changes everything. You know that, right?" Adam asked.

"I'm afraid to guess at what the Marshall might have done. He didn't exactly encourage peace around here." Brax issued a sharp sigh.

"No, he did not."

7

P rudence rubbed her eyes and grabbed her glasses. The sun was up, peaking through the drawn curtains. She felt around on the bed, searching for Adam as she put them on. The bed was cold where he used to be. She shot up and checked the crib. Angel was gone.

Rubbing blurry eyes, she realized that she had her memories from yesterday. Though the days before were still a blank. She had no idea if she would ever get those back. Either way, this was progress. Excitement bubbled up as she glanced around.

Adam had to be here somewhere. She slipped out of the covers. At the foot of the bed, her clothes were clean, stacked, and folded. She grabbed them before freshening up in the bathroom and changing, realizing she had underestimated the power of clean clothes her entire life.

There was a brush in the top drawer, so she used it to try to tame her curls. *Good luck there.*

With a much more positive outlook, she headed downstairs. The house was quiet, too quiet, and the unsettled feeling returned. She tiptoed into the kitchen where she saw

Angel making cooing noises at Adam as he held her with one arm while standing at the window.

She cleared her throat, not wanting to catch him off guard.

He immediately turned around.

"Morning," he said, and she could have sworn she caught him studying her. Did he wonder about her memory too?

"The sun's up already," she said with a thumbs up. "Thanks for letting me sleep."

"Figured you needed the rest," he said. "Plus, me and Angel have been getting to know each other."

"I'm guessing there's no word from the sheriff yet," she said.

He shook his head. She figured as much. He would have led with the update.

"May I?" She walked right over to him, resisting the urge to press up to her tiptoes and plant a kiss on those perfect lips of his. She really did get a good night's sleep if she was aching to kiss Adam before coffee. But then he was that bone-melting hot.

"Be my guest." He handed over the baby, who raised an immediate objection to the transfer.

An emotion she couldn't quite pinpoint darkened his eyes when he looked at Angel.

"This should help." He cut across to the table and then returned with the binky.

The little girl took it, and immediately settled down. Prudence took note of how good he was becoming with her. Not for the first time did she wonder if he was somehow the child's father. The hair color was right. The eyes were wrong. But who could really tell with a baby this young?

"How about coffee?" he asked, breaking into the train of thought before it could gain too much steam.

"Sounds like heaven to me," she admitted.

"You remember," he whispered as he walked past and there was more than a hint of relief in his voice.

Prudence looked onto the expansive backyard. The grass was mostly green with plenty of bald patches, thanks to a lack of rain for almost two years running. If they didn't get rain soon, it would mean trouble for crops and cattle. Even so, the landscape was like something out of a postcard. The twin barns off in the distance might be reminders of a divided family, but they were magnificent against the backdrop of dozens of mesquite trees.

"I'll just put this on the table for whenever you're ready," Adam said.

She immediately made her way over. Beautiful as the place was, she needed a caffeine boost. She took a seat and cradled Angel with one arm. The first sip was always the best, Prudence thought, welcoming the burn on her throat.

"Are you hungry?" Adam asked.

"I can't eat before I wake up. But thank you," she said, taking in the massive kitchen. There was an oversized gas stovetop with two ovens, all stainless steel. More counter space than she imagined being able to use in a week, let alone for one day's worth of cooking. She'd seen fully staffed restaurant kitchens smaller than this one.

"What is it?" Adam asked, taking a seat next to her.

She shot her best confused look at him.

"Your forehead wrinkles when you're thinking hard about something. I'm curious what that is," he said.

A trill of awareness skittered across her skin at his perusal.

"I was just taking it all in and thinking how lonely it

must have been to live in this massive space all by himself." She took another sip and smiled down at the bundle in her arms.

"The Marshall didn't seem to mind. In fact, he probably enjoyed the irony," he said.

"Seems like a shame. I can imagine lively dinners here at this table and holiday meals that make my mouth water just thinking about them. Fresh baked cookies would be cooling over there and the smell of ham and turkey with cornbread dressing would fill the room." She caught herself spelling out the fantasy and her cheeks warmed.

"What you're describing would have been nice. Firebrands just don't work that way," he said matter-of-fact, but she picked up on a note of sadness he seemed intent to cover. Or maybe he was just resigned to the childhood he'd had. He was on to something there, though. She'd learned a long time ago that it was impossible to go back and change the past.

"Did something happen to make him so hardened?" She couldn't help but wonder what his grandfather's story was and why he would push everyone away. Her first hint that he wasn't a warm-and-fuzzy type came with the fact he had his grandchildren call him the Marshall instead of something endearing like granddad or grandpa.

"I have no idea. He wasn't the kind of person who discussed his feelings." Adam covered his disappointment with a smile.

"That makes it hard to get to know someone," she said, liking that he was talking to her about something important to him. And she sensed the lack of relationship with his grandfather hit him harder than he wanted to admit.

"The crazy part is that all I ever wanted from him was to be able to sit down one day and have a beer together. Talk about my grandmother, who I barely knew, or what they were like growing up. How he knew she was *the one*. Or we could've talked about why he cared about cattle ranching so much. Hell, I don't care. Having the beer and talking one-on-one was all that mattered. What we would have said wasn't so important." He paused, shifting his gaze toward the window. "Now, I'll never get the chance. That's the part I hate. He'll always be a mystery to me, and we no longer have any chance at a relationship. I keep thinking maybe I should have tried harder. He was healthy, though. I thought there was time," he admitted. "Or at least he seemed so."

"He's a fool for missing out on getting to know you if you ask my opinion," Prudence didn't miss a beat.

Adam stared at the window for a long moment. Then, he broke into a wide smile in a show of perfectly white, perfectly straight teeth. "His loss, I guess."

"Yes, it is," she confirmed, happy to see him smile and look like he meant it.

"I still would've liked to have had the beer," he said, raising his coffee cup instead.

"He's a fool for not suggesting it. No disrespect intended," she quickly qualified. "And I'll have a beer with you anytime you want."

Adam rewarded her with a sincere look and another smile that made her bones liquefy. "Thank you. I needed that."

"I'm not sure what I did to deserve thanks, but you're welcome." All she was doing was stating the truth. The bold offer of a having a beer anytime wasn't something she would normally do. She was getting more comfortable in her skin and with her new bravado.

"How about breakfast now?" he asked, pushing off the table with one hand.

"Do you have toast?" she asked.

"And jam," he said, turning long enough to fire off a wink.

"Sold." Prudence wasn't much of a breakfast eater. In fact, she normally downed a couple of bites of yogurt to get her pills down. Which reminded her, "I need to get home soon."

"We can leave right after you eat." Adam made quick work of toast. He had a plate to her with twin Texas-sized slices of bread smattered in jam. She normally ate hers with a dab of butter. After taking the first bite, she would never be able to go back.

"How long do we have until she needs another bottle?" she asked.

"She had one a few minutes before you came down, so we should be good until noon," he supplied.

He sure had the routine down in a short time. She glanced at the baby. *Where is your mother, sweet girl?*

And the question burning in the back of her mind that wouldn't let up. *Who is your father?*

ADAM BORROWED a car seat from Casey, who already had it strapped in the back seat of the truck by the time him and Prudence were ready to leave. He'd already programmed Prudence's address into his phone's GPS, so after brief instructions on proper car seat usage, Adam was on the road.

Prudence's house was smack in the center of town. Some of the earliest settlers in Lone Star Pass were from Germany and they did their best to recreate home, or so his grandmother had told him. The downtown area was a blend of

Gothic and Romanesque architecture built after a major city. He couldn't remember which one and figured he should have paid better attention when his grandmother spoke. But then he had a lot of regrets when it came to what he should have done while she was alive. She was the talker between her and the Marshall, and loved to sing. Those were the few memories he had of her.

Speaking of his grandfather, had he always been so stern? Or had he become that way after his wife died? Adam couldn't remember. All he knew was the man had married two other times. Had one divorce under his belt and buried his third wife two years ago. He had a reputation for being a ladies' man despite being a married man. Adam could never be certain when that had started.

He glanced at the clock as he pulled in front of the two-story. There were lines of cars parked on either side of the street. He navigated through them, making sure he didn't lose a side-mirror in the process. Being in town always made him want to loosen his collar.

It had taken an hour to get to Prudence's house. She woke after eight this morning and they spent more than half an hour in the kitchen talking and drinking coffee. It would take another hour to drive back. They would need to be on the road in about an hour if they wanted to get home before the next feeding time.

Adam was realizing how much the early weeks of parenting were about being on a tight schedule and life revolving around bottles of formula.

"Think we need to bring in the diaper bag?" he asked.

"Never hurts since the diapers are in there," she said, motioning toward the back seat. "In fact, I'm surprised she hasn't—"

"Oh, she did. Four o'clock in the morning. Brax helped

with clean up," he said, wrinkling his nose just thinking about it.

"Bad memory?" she teased, her voice playful.

"Let's just say I'm not taking the next one," he shot back.

Prudence laughed. She exited the truck before he had a chance to get around and open the door for her. Call him old-fashioned but he would always offer.

She had the baby out of the car seat with a flick of her thumb. Since he wanted to be useful, he offered to take the diaper bag.

"Actually, do you mind holding her? Now that I think about it, I don't have a key with me so I'll have to go around back for the spare," she said.

He shouldered the diaper bag and then took the baby. It wasn't logical but she felt even smaller to him out here and he was suddenly afraid he would drop her.

"I'll be a second," Prudence said.

"I'd rather go with you, if you don't mind." He didn't want either of these two out of his sight.

She glanced around before nodding. "Do you want me to carry something?"

"Nope. I got it." He was getting more comfortable holding the baby outside.

As they passed the front porch, the squeak of a screen door caused his fight response to kick into high gear. A male figure sprinted away from the back of her house.

Prudence muttered the same curse he was thinking.

"Can you take her?" he asked.

She nodded as he handed Angel over.

"Stick as close to me as you can." Adam was fast. He didn't doubt his abilities there. But if he took off in a full sprint, he'd be leaving Prudence and the baby alone. So, basically, this situation was a no-win. Leave her and he would be leaving her vulnerable. Stay and the jerk who'd been inside her home would get away.

Adam ate up the real estate to the backyard, keeping Prudence close. He scanned the area. A series of chain link fences gave him plenty of visibility, but no one was outside. Not a homeowner. Not a kid. Not a dog.

Bad luck, he thought as tires squealed out front.

Adam jogged toward his truck. Again, a few seconds too late to see anything in between the vehicles. By the time he made it to the street, the vehicle had turned, and the dogs had caught on. He fished his cell out of his pocket and called the sheriff to the backdrop of howling and barking.

Lawler answered on the first ring. He sounded pre-occupied. Adam wasted no time giving the lawman an update.

"I'll be right there," Lawler said. "Don't touch anything."

"We'll wait inside the truck," Adam promised, figuring it was too dangerous to stand here in the middle of the street. He quickly added, "Prudence remembers."

"How much?" Lawler's tone held out a lot of hope.

"What we already know. But I think it's significant she woke up with those memories," Adam said.

"I agree," Lawler said. "Now, to figure out why she has the memory lapses in the first place."

"How long before you get here?" Adam was already calculating bottles and timelines in the back of his mind. This would set back their schedule. They would have to stick around long enough for another bottle. Plus, Angel had been wrapped like a burrito all night. Maybe they could take her out and let her play on the floor. Or whatever babies this age did. And, of course, depending on the state of Prudence's house. The perp didn't have anything in his hands but that didn't mean he didn't destroy the place.

"Forty minutes with lights and sirens to clear the path,"

Lawler said. "I have a deputy closer. I can send him over to dust for prints on the door handles."

"Sounds good," Adam said.

"We can talk about the next steps once I get there," Lawler said. There was an ominous quality to his tone that didn't sit well with Adam.

"Okay," he said casually, trying not to alert Prudence to his concern at what Lawler meant by that.

The sheriff's statement had been a loaded one. Adam didn't want to guess what it meant, because in every scenario he could think of, this little girl was taken away. A surprising amount of anger roiled through him at the thought.

8

"Is Lawler coming?" Prudence had only caught one side of the conversation. Despite Adam being cool on the phone, her stress levels climbed. There was something about his expression and careful choice of words that distressed her.

"Yes." He placed his hand on the small of her back, and a trill of awareness shot through her. The world could be crashing down around her and that man's touch would still elicit a response from her body. He urged her toward the truck and it dawned on her why. *Safety.*

"My purse might be in there. My cell phone," she said. The fact her home had been broken into made her feel violated. And angry. She had no idea where this new bravado came from, but she couldn't imagine going back to her old timid self.

"We'll get both of them if they are," he reassured, his voice a study in calm. One look into his eyes said he'd fight with his bare hands if anyone touched Angel.

A father's instinct?

"And Lawler is sending a deputy over right away," he continued.

As if to punctuate his sentence, she heard the sound of a siren wailing in the distance. It did little to calm her rattled nerves. The baby woke, blinking her eyes open as Adam helped Prudence into the passenger seat. Prudence was surprised Angel had slept through the dog racket.

"Scoot over," he said, climbing in right behind her. He locked the doors, a stark reminder of the danger they were in. Then, he unlocked and opened the glove box. He palmed a handgun. "If the jerk comes back, he won't get away so easily."

The thought of the creep returning caused all of Prudence's protective instincts to flare. One look into the little girl's eyes and Prudence realized how much trouble she was in. If she was smart, she'd keep an emotional distance. The sheriff would find Angel's rightful parents and she would be taken back home. Of course, that was the best-case scenario for all involved. So why did the thought cause an ache the size of the Gulf of Mexico to park itself inside her chest?

She didn't even like babies.

Angel was an exception, of course. But still. The thought of having a child of her own had always sounded worse than a root canal.

Adam kept watch, surveying the area while they waited for the deputy to show. How messed up was that? Prudence didn't have much but what she had was paid for. She thought about any valuables the jerk could have been stealing. Her laptop came to mind. She'd be lost without it. Her phone. She had credit cards and a little bit of money.

Most of her decorations comprised of art she'd created

or items she'd picked up and refurbished from antique shops. There wasn't anything worth much, except to her. Everything she'd worked for was inside those walls. Everything she'd built on her own after teen years that had kicked her butt.

And yet, right now, her main focus was keeping the baby safe. Maternal instincts she never realize she had kicked in, telling her to keep the baby in her arms safe, happy, and alive. Prudence had never felt a more powerful instinct. Was this how all mothers felt? It made her think about her own and miss her so much it physically hurt.

The wailing siren grew louder until a deputy's vehicle roared up beside them. Angel frowned, her chin quivered, and she wound up for a good cry.

A young-ish guy stepped out of the marked SUV dressed in the same tan button-down shirt Lawler had on last night. At least Prudence's memory seemed to be intact other than a blank spot where three days should be.

Adam slipped out of the truck and met the deputy in the street. She watched as he explained what had gone down. He pointed toward the backyard. It occurred to her that she left a key in an obvious spot, in a colorful planter. But then, half the reason she'd moved back to Lone Star Pass after losing her family was for safety reasons. It had been many years since she'd been that teen who'd been muted by a horrific act. No one got to make her go back to that place in her thoughts again. She bit back a curse. No one should get to disrupt her life again.

Speaking of which, she needed to go inside and take her meds. The new pill her doctor recommended needed to be taken at the same time every day.

Angel belted out a pitiful-sounding cry. Prudence

checked the time. It was too early for a bottle. "What's wrong, sweet girl?"

If only Angel could speak. How easy would that make this? Because this whole feeling helpless bit was for the birds.

The binky. Where was the pacifier? Then again, maybe it was healthier to let the girl cry. Her life had been turned upside-down in an instant. Prudence wished she could join Angel. She hadn't cried in longer than she could remember. There were times when she wished she could, like now. Just to let it all out. Her emotions had been bottled up.

Survival mechanism, her first therapist had explained. Apparently, Prudence had become an expert at it.

The next thing she knew the deputy went back to his vehicle and Adam opened the passenger door.

"Deputy Smithfield is going to start at the back of the house, since that's where most home invaders work," he explained.

"The key's back there. I made it easy for him," she said. Now, she needed to think about having an alarm system installed. She would definitely put the key back on her ring. There were a few other security measures running through her thoughts. Again, she thought about getting a dog of her own.

As much as she loved the idea, she had to put her clients first. Having a dog meant responsibilities beyond taking care of herself, a task she was most definitely not ready for. Plus, what would she do with said dog while she had overnight jobs, which many of hers were?

This wasn't the first time she'd had to be reasonable rather than go with her heart. Even though caring for other people's pets made her want her own that much more.

"Don't beat yourself up. Everyone in town leaves a key somewhere outside their house. We don't even lock doors at the ranch, and half the time I go to the feed store I leave my keys in the floorboard of the truck," he said.

"Well, that makes me feel better." Plus, the baby had settled down without a binky, thanks to Prudence's gentle bouncing. There was something very satisfying about the accomplishment.

"We should be able to go inside in a few minutes. Survey the damage," Adam said.

"Good. I'm not supposed to get behind on my medication." A part of her dreaded walking into her home. The other side needed to see what she would be dealing with.

DEPUTY SMITHFIELD PEERED around the side of the house and waved Adam over. He exited the truck first and scanned the street before indicating it was safe for Prudence and Angel to follow.

Around back of the house, he immediately noted the glass break. She had one of those glass paneled doors that let in a lot of light, but he imagined it would be a burglar's dream.

"Careful where you walk," Deputy Smithfield said after introducing himself to Prudence.

"I will," she said with resolve. "He didn't bother checking for a key."

"My guess is that he was in a hurry," Smithfield said.

"A smash and grab job?" This couldn't be a coincidence.

"It looks that way," Smithfield said with a shrug. "We'll know more once Ms. Owens goes inside and takes inventory of her belongings."

"There was nothing obvious in his hands when he took off that way." Adam pointed east.

"Do you have any medications?" Smithfield asked Prudence.

"Oh, right. Yes. Nothing that would have street value but you just reminded me I need to take my new prescription." She motioned toward the door before catching Adam's gaze. "Will you come with me so I can manage the baby?"

He nodded and then followed her inside. *Her new prescription?* The words stuck in the back of his mind. She'd mentioned needing to take meds before. Had she mentioned the prescription was new?

"Do you remember going to the doctor recently?" Adam noticed there didn't seem to be anything out of place in the kitchen. It was cozy and tidy. Everything had a place. Her laptop sat on the eat-in table.

"I went a couple of weeks ago," she said. "Why?"

"The medication. I thought you said it was a new prescription." He followed her up a stairwell to the second story. There was a small landing and four doors. Two of those led to bedrooms. He could easily see because the doors were open. The third went to a shared bathroom. These old houses didn't have en suites.

"It is." She stopped at the sink of the small bathroom and opened the cabinet. There was a sink, a commode, and a clawfoot tub that had been modernized with a shower option. She grabbed a bottle and shook. It rattled.

"I'm confused," he admitted. "How long have you been taking the new pills?"

She started to open her mouth and then stopped. Realization dawned.

"Three days," she said. "My doctor didn't say anything about memory loss being a side effect. I read the paper that comes with it and I can promise there was no mention of it there."

"What about conflicts? What are the pills for?" he asked.

"They're antianxiety meds," she said, her cheeks tinting with embarrassment. She added, "Although, I haven't felt like I needed them lately."

There was a sad story behind that prescription. He'd be willing to bet money on it. His respect for her grew even more at the fact she was willing to face it. Getting help wasn't a sign of weakness, not in his eyes.

"Mind if I have a look in your medicine cabinet?" he asked.

"Be my guest." She took a step back and started gently bouncing Angel.

He examined the labels on three bottles, keeping his gaze on the pills and not the other contents—contents that weren't any of his business otherwise.

"I'm no expert but since the days match up, there must be a bad interaction going on with one of these," he stated.

"It's crazy because I felt like I'd been doing better on my own when I ran out of my old prescription. My doctor said she'd consider taking one off the list if I'd agree to go to counseling, which I haven't had time for," she said.

"She's probably covering her backside with the insurance company." He'd heard worse.

Prudence issued a sharp sigh.

"We can call the drugstore to check. I had to go to a specialty pharmacist to have this one made,"' she said. "I can promise you that I'm not taking that one again."

A burst of pride filled his chest at the possibility they'd figured out a viable reason for her memory loss. Better yet, it was temporary.

"When did you stop your last pills?" he asked, not wanting her to get her body in trouble if she needed them.

"It's been more than thirty days. I'd secretly started weaning myself for the past six months. I had a feeling my doctor wouldn't like it, so I didn't tell her." She shrugged a shoulder.

"You should be safe then if you skip a dose." Adam had no plans to tempt fate. He fished his cell out of his pocket and, after ten minutes on the phone, confirmed two of her medications were known for causing a reaction.

"No more of these." She started to throw the medication into the trash. He stopped her.

"Hold onto those to show to Lawler. He'll need the names for his report, and it is evidence in case Angel's case ends up in trial." He couldn't imagine a scenario where she would be anything but a witness.

"Right," she said with a new spark in her eye, like she'd been vindicated.

"Is anything missing in here?" he asked. This development was welcomed news. He'd believed in her without needing an explanation. Seeing her relief stirred his chest.

She checked the cabinet out before shaking her head.

"I'd like to take a walk around the place. I already noticed my laptop sitting on the kitchen table where I must have left it," she said.

"Do you want me to hold Angel?" He was so much more comfortable in a surprisingly short amount of time. Those first few hours with her had been the equivalent of drinking from a firehose. It amazed him how quickly he'd picked it up. And Prudence was incredible with Angel too, a real natural.

She handed over the baby and then moved from room to

room, taking a mental inventory and pointing out anything of value.

"Most everything I own is sentimental. Something I made or refurbished. It was therapeutic when my parents and sister…" she flashed nervous eyes at him before continuing, "were killed."

"I'm so sorry," he said, his heart truly went out to her.

"I was there in the room, blindfolded. He forced me to listen and said he was going oldest to youngest. When it was my turn, the neighbor's dog, who was always getting loose, ran through our dog door. The neighbor followed, interrupting the killings." She closed her eyes and her body tensed. "He's in jail for the rest of his life, by the way. Justice served."

Those last two words were hollow, and he understood why. They couldn't bring her family back. He walked over to her and took her hand in his after securing the little girl in the carrier. The urge to kiss Prudence, tell her everything would be okay, and find a way to ease her pain was a physical ache.

"I was nine years old when it happened," she continued. "Came here to live with an aunt and uncle after. They were great. Took me to a good psychiatrist in Austin for years every Saturday. Enrolled me in school when I was finally brave enough to leave the house again."

He squeezed her fingers for reassurance, for comfort.

"And now you're the only non-medical professional or blood relative I've ever spoken to about it." She opened her eyes, those lakes of blue seeing right through him.

"Requesting permission to kiss you now," he said.

"Permission granted." She pushed up to her tiptoes and met him halfway.

He pressed his lips to hers gently.

"I think you're incredibly brave," he said, his mouth moving against hers.

She brought her hands to his arms, digging her fingernails in as she teased his tongue inside her mouth.

He pulled back enough to say, "And beautiful."

In that moment, he realized he was in too deep.

9

"Are you upstairs, Adam?"

Sheriff Lawler's voice cut into the moment happening between Adam and Prudence. With great effort, she pulled back first. He opened those incredible coral-sea blue eyes, and she knew she was in trouble.

"Coming," he said, and his voice was gruff.

"Go on down and talk to him. I'll be right there," she said, needing a minute to pull herself together.

Adam leaned in for one more kiss and it literally curled her toes. Talking to him about her family had been so freeing, like a weight had been lifted off her shoulders.

"I'll fill him in on the medication combination," he said. "Do you want me to take her downstairs?"

She nodded, needing time to catch her breath there too. Her mind had been filled with images of her, Adam, and Angel living together as a family, and that wasn't going to happen. Angel already had parents out there. Prudence would never try to stand in the way of a reunion.

Adam disappeared down the stairs as Prudence tried to will her pulse back to normal. Her heart beat against her ribcage, hammering out its own frantic rhythm. Breathing was already difficult, so when she thought about the inevitable moment they would hand Angel over to Sheriff Lawler, pain tightened her chest.

Angel deserved to be with her parents no matter how attached Prudence was becoming. She needed to get a grip. Moving into the bathroom, she stopped at the sink to splash cold water on her face.

There, she was already feeling better. She teased a comb through her kinky hair as best she could. Lot of good that did and there was no time to straighten it with an iron. In times like these, it was best to embrace the curls. She dabbed gel on her hand before rubbing her palms together. Slicking it through her hair helped.

She grabbed her small tin of tinted lip gloss. She tapped her pinky finger inside and then circled her lips a couple of times—lips that were still swollen from Adam's kisses. The man was a good kisser. Beyond good. In fact, that was the most electric kiss she'd ever experienced.

Dating had been tricky given her background. Prudence had powered through the first couple, checking her watch every time her dates looked away. Just like anything, time and practice helped her improve. Meeting new people had always been a trigger. Maybe it was because she knew Fallon, but Prudence felt nothing but comfortable around Adam despite how the air crackled from their chemistry.

A few deep breaths and a little eyeliner made her feel human again. She resisted the urge to change clothes since the ones she had on were clean. She wanted to get downstairs and hear what Lawler had to say.

Lawler and Adam were standing in the kitchen when she joined them. Deputy Smithfield must have gotten what he needed because he was nowhere to be seen. Relief washed over her that none of her valuables were missing.

Except her car, purse, and cell phone.

With her laptop, her cell phone would be easy enough to track. If she were lucky, she'd hit the jackpot of locating all three.

"Morning," Lawler said.

"Same to you." Prudence didn't like the look on his face. "Would you like to sit down? I can fix a cup of coffee."

"No, thanks." He held a shaky hand up. "I've had four cups already. Any more and I'm afraid I'll cause an earthquake."

She smiled.

"I'll take you up on the offer to sit, though." He walked over to the kitchen table and pulled out a chair. "Adam just filled me in about the medication interaction."

"It's such a relief to know and be able to stop the blackouts," she admitted, taking a seat in front of her laptop. Was that also the reason for her new bravado? It was a bravado she planned to hang onto.

"I can imagine so," Lawler said as Adam joined them.

She looked around. "Nothing seems to be missing. Except, of course, my cell, purse, and car. I'm guessing I had those with me. So, I doubt they had anything to do with the burglary."

Lawler shook his head and gave an ominous look that caught Prudence's full attention. She compressed her lips together and didn't hide a frown.

"I don't think this is a coincidence," he started.

"Why not?" She had her own obvious reasons for questioning the timing too. She wanted to hear him out first.

"Burglars usually go the easy route. They're in and out, stealing you blind before you know it," he said and then paused. "I suspect this perp and his cohorts were waiting for you to come home."

"Could he be someone I know?" Didn't that make the hairs on the back of her neck prickle? Thinking someone familiar to her would break inside her home and wait for her return sent an icy chill down her back.

"I'm not ruling out the possibility. This person might know you from a distance, on social media, or through a work acquaintance," he said.

"He came for her, right?" She motioned toward Angel.

"That's my hunch," he said. The thought made her skin crawl.

"So, they figured out where I live," she whispered, stating mere fact. "Does that mean they'll come back?"

"It's possible." He drummed his fingers on the table. "Probable."

"My aunt and uncle sold their place a couple of years ago to be close to her sister in Houston, so that's not an option. I can stay in a motel or something until this is cleared up." This was nothing like the crime against her parents, and yet that same dark-cloud feeling engulfed her.

"You can stay with me at the ranch. Hell, the main house is empty. You could have it to yourself," Adam interjected.

"That might be a good idea," Lawler said.

Letting someone cause her to run away from her own home burned her from the inside out. She wouldn't be stupid, though. She'd grit her teeth and take the safest action. "Okay."

Lawler nodded, like he understood the sacrifice she would be making before turning his attention toward Adam. "There's more."

Adam picked up a pencil sitting on the table and rolled it around his fingers. "She needs a security system and—"

"It's about your ex." Lawler shot an apologetic look toward Prudence like he'd picked up on the attraction running between them. She had no designs on Adam. He was helping her through a rough patch. That was all. They'd kissed a couple of times. Their emotions were most likely heightened since she'd been in danger. An annoying voice in the back of her mind called her out on the oversimplification. Her heart disagreed with the assessment despite logic trying to intervene and convince her their chemistry was circumstantial.

"What about her?" Adam let go of the pencil. It tumbled onto the table and rolled before coming to a stop against the saltshaker.

"I checked on her to see where she was and how she was doing," Lawler said.

The implication sitting in the room was that he didn't trust Adam's story. He reached for the pencil, this time keeping a firm grip on it. Adam's gaze narrowed and his lips thinned. Was he over her?

"I apologize for being the one to have to tell you this," Lawler hedged. Hemming and hawing only served to increase Adam's tension. She could see it in the taut muscles of his face.

"Spit it out. I'm a grown man and we broke up almost a year ago," Adam said. It occurred to her that he was expecting to hear engagement or marriage news. He tensed like a prizefighter preparing to take a punch.

"Her parents identified her body." Lawler stopped there as though taking a lighter approach might somehow soften the blow.

The pencil cracked under Adam's grip.

"How did it happen? When?" A mix of anger and shock

laced his tone. There was another emotion present too. Disbelief?

"According to the coroner's report, she was strangled sometime between four and six days ago," Lawler said. He lowered his head before adding, "I'm sorry for the loss."

Murder?

A gasp escaped before Prudence had a chance to bring her hand up to cover. Half a dozen questions sprang to mind. Was Libby in an abusive relationship? For how long? Had she been forced to refuse Adam's proposal in some way?

Prudence reached across the table to touch Adam in a show of support. He immediately withdrew. The broken pencil slammed into the table as he smacked his hand down.

Angel started fussing as realization rammed Prudence like a head-on collision. One question floated to the surface...was Adam a father?

⟿

THIS NEWS CHANGED everything for Adam.

"Does Angel belong to her?" he asked.

"Yes," Lawler said.

Adam knew what the sheriff's next question would be. "I still don't believe I'm the father."

"I know," Lawler said. "And we don't have to take a sample or do any tests. The most important one is seeing if we can tie the little girl to Elizabeth."

"Libby," Adam corrected.

"She went by Libby. Her full name is..." Lawler flashed eyes at Adam, "*was* Elizabeth Sue Warrington."

"Warrington? Isn't that a prominent Houston family?" he asked.

"Yes," Lawler responded.

"She told me her last name was Daniels." He was certain he'd seen identification as such. "I was never told that," he conceded, wondering what else she'd hidden.

"There are signs when someone's had a baby," Prudence chimed in.

"Obviously," Lawler agreed. "It's the reason I'd like to run the test."

Prudence compressed her lips in a frown. She looked at the baby with the most tender expression.

Despite the breakup, hearing Libby was dead hit him in a dark place. She was too young, too vibrant. Looking back, she might not have been right for him and she seemed to have sense enough to know it, but he didn't wish this on her. Losing his grandfather was difficult, but the Marshall had lived a full life. Libby's had barely even begun. The unfairness of it fisted his hands. No life should be cut short from senseless violence, especially not someone with her whole life ahead of her.

Angel wiggled in his lap and he could have sworn the little girl could sense his mood shift. She'd gone from happy and contented to fussy and agitated in a matter of seconds.

"I can feed her," Prudence offered.

Adam nodded.

She took a turn fixing the bottle and he handed over the baby, still reeling from the news. And what if Libby was Angel's mother? What then? What would happen to the little girl?

"She was secretive about her family," he said to Lawler after reclaiming his seat. "Told me they didn't get along and she rarely spoke to them. Was that true?"

"I have a deputy over there speaking to them right now. You know I can't comment on an ongoing murder investigation," Lawler said.

"I'm just trying to figure out how much of our relationship was a lie." To think he'd planned to spend the rest of his life with someone who'd kept her identity from him. It seemed like something out of a TV show, not real life. Not *his* life. How did Libby get one over on him for almost a year of dating?

Job hazard, he thought. He worked long hours on the ranch. Animals needed care seven days a week. He'd been covering for Casey during his wife's pregnancy, so they could spend more time together. And then there was his aversion to all things social media. The only reason he ever turned on a screen was to watch an occasional game. It was easy to have as background noise when he was at his home. He wasn't much on surfing the internet and Libby had almost always come to him after the initial few months of dating. There'd been a dinner out when he'd almost gone face-down at the table during calving season.

Looking back, he realized it took a special person to want to be a rancher's wife. She would have to be real comfortable being alone for long periods of time, and happy to stay in rather than go out much of the time. Libby had come to him, but he'd sensed she was getting bored with staying in.

Considering he didn't know her real last name, he couldn't take much of their relationship on face value. Was she spending time with him to hide out from an ex? Was she seeing someone else during their relationship? What about her folks? Did they know about him as she'd said? Or had she kept him a secret from them too?

Adam stood up and paced around the room as anger surfaced. "What do you need for a DNA test?"

He didn't believe he was Angel's father. However, he needed to put the question to rest.

"Swab of the inside of your cheek," Lawler said. "And hers."

"Simple enough." Adam made another lap. Now, he needed to know who had targeted Prudence. Was it the same person who'd killed Libby? The coincidence would be...

Right. The only connection was him. Libby lived in Austin where they'd met on a weekend when he'd gone to hear his favorite low-key country band play, Bottoms Up Red, featuring a local girl done good, Raleigh Perry.

Libby had caught his eye. She was a beautiful woman with her long blonde hair and green eyes. She'd put on more makeup than he thought she needed, the complete opposite of Prudence who barely wore any.

The pink gloss on her lips called attention to her creamy skin. But he was supposed to be thinking about Libby. She had always been dressed to the nines. Hair done up and always wearing heels. She'd been a little too slick for him in the beginning with her bronzed skin and California beach body. In fact, he'd nicknamed her California in the early days. It had taken a month for her to finally pluck up the courage to ask him not to call her by that name.

Strange thinking about it now, considering she'd lied about the very thing she was upset about. He didn't know her last name.

"She had a fake ID with a different last name on it," Adam told Lawler.

The lawman perked up at the news.

"Oh yeah?" he asked.

"Daniels. Her ID said Libby Daniels," Adam supplied. He couldn't help but think about Prudence's raw honesty. Her simple beauty had drawn him in. She didn't feel the need to cover up her true self. He'd liked that about her instantly. He also never would have described a pair of sweatpants as sexy before, except that was what he thought when she had them on.

Still, he had no plans to act on his attraction to Prudence. The couple of white-hot kisses they'd shared were the end of it. Period. Whatever was going on between them needed to be cut off right then and there before someone got hurt.

His job required all of his attention. His grandfather had just passed away. His time was already committed to the family and the ranch.

Speaking of being so tired he could barely remember his name, it dawned on him that Libby had stopped by after the breakup. Once. They'd had breakup sex. He'd insisted on using a condom, like always, but the possibility Angel was his child could no longer be denied.

10

———

Prudence put two-and-two together, realizing what Adam seemed to be in denial about. He and his ex broke off their relationship less than a year ago. There were fifty-two weeks in a year. It took forty to have a baby. His fatherhood depended on the timeline of their breakup.

Her heart went out to the little girl who would never know her mother. The writing was on the wall about Libby. She had possibly even scribbled the note for someone to get her baby to Adam moments before dying.

How awful was that?

Other inevitable questions followed. Was she trying to get her baby to a man who she knew would protect her? Or was she simply trying to unite a baby with her father?

As Prudence gazed at the sweet little girl who seemed so content taking down her bottle, her heart literally bled at her loss. At least she'd had nine years with her family. It might not be much, but she had a couple of memories she clung to and a box of family photos in the attic she didn't have the heart to bring down.

Prudence's mind reeled. She knew what it was like to grow up without a mother. She'd been so young when she lost hers that she barely remembered her. Her aunt and uncle rarely spoke about Prudence's parents. Now, she realized it had probably been hard on them too. They were good people and it had been such a tragedy. Prudence had developed a stutter, that had taken years to overcome, and it had been part of the reason she'd kept to herself during her school years.

Her aunt had had a cat named Percy. Percy was a fancy Himalayan with more white fur than Prudence had ever seen. The cat would sit at the foot of Prudence's bed while she read out loud, her aunt's idea. It had been a stroke of brilliance too. Reading to Percy didn't make Prudence feel self-conscious when the words wouldn't come out right. She'd developed two loves during those years, animals and reading.

Even now, Prudence preferred a quiet night at home or with other people's pets to going out to some splashy restaurant or loud bar. She'd always been a solitary person, long before the tragedy.

There'd always been enough in Lone Star Pass to keep her active and busy. The move to Austin had been harder on her. First of all, living downtown was like being locked inside one of those ant farms. Everyone seemed to be crawling on top of each other, trying to climb somewhere... anywhere else. A memory that stuck out was being on Lake Travis over Memorial Day weekend. Her parents had rented two double kayaks but the wake from passing boats made it next to impossible to go anywhere. Ten minutes into the hour rental, they'd returned to shore.

She glanced down at Angel. Right then and there she promised to be there for the little girl much in the way her own aunt and uncle had been there for her. Without them, Prudence had no idea how she would have turned out.

But then, being a Firebrand would give Angel all the family she could handle. Prudence couldn't help but muse there was a lot of testosterone over there on the family's ranch. She knew of Adam's mother even though she didn't know the woman personally. Was he close to his parents? Based on what he'd said so far, she didn't think so.

There was so much the two of them didn't know about each other. And yet, she could have sworn she saw her entire life flash before her eyes when they'd first met. A life together. A future.

How wild was that?

She chalked it up to residual effects of the medication. Real love developed over time, between two people who knew each other. Yet what she felt with Adam was stronger than anything she'd experienced. An attraction like a planet pulling the sun toward it. And, yes, she'd thought about how amazing he must be in bed considering how well he knew how to work his tongue. But that was physical. This was so much more than that.

There was no way she could ignore how much she was drawn to the man.

Bottle finished, Prudence burped the baby before excusing herself to change her diaper in the living room. At this rate, they would run out of diapers soon. At least the feeding would buy them a few more hours to figure out their next move. She looked around, thinking how much she hated that jerk who'd broken into her house, for violating her safe haven. Most folks in town left their doors unlocked. She'd always been careful. Seeing how easy it was to violate her home caused a streak of anger a mile wide to course through her.

No one got to take her sense of security away from her again. *No one,* she repeated to herself for emphasis.

Looking at Angel, she couldn't help but think she'd go to the ends of the earth to ensure the baby never experienced that kind of fear. Prudence caught herself. She was being overprotective over a child that wasn't even hers.

When had this little girl wiggled her way into Prudence's heart?

FROM ADAM'S vantage point in the kitchen, he kept one eye on Prudence and Angel as he waited for Lawler to return with a DNA test kit. He sat there, tapping his fingers on the table, an uneasy feeling gripping him.

It was impossible to imagine Libby dead. His hands fisted, anger surged, and he scanned the room in search of an easy outlet. Their relationship might not have worked out, but damn. He didn't wish death on his worst enemy. He searched his brain for the timing of their breakup sex. The time period was a still fuzzy considering it had been during calving season but had to be at least a few weeks after she walked away. They'd been together roughly eight weeks shy of a year.

Again, he smacked the flat of his palm on the tabletop.

The back door opened, and Lawler walked in. There were two kits in hand. He sidestepped a patch of broken glass on his way over. Adam figured he could clean up the shards once Lawler joined Prudence and Angel in the living room to collect her sample.

It didn't take two minutes for the sheriff to take Adam's DNA.

Adam glanced in the next room and his chest squeezed

at watching Prudence play with the baby. Angel was on top of her blanket on the floor, her arms and legs kicking and punching. The sounds of her cooing nearly did him in.

So, the kid was cute. Didn't mean she belonged to him.

He stood up and grabbed the broom leaning against the back door. The perp could have used it to break the window. He reminded himself to tell Prudence not to leave anything outside that could be used as a weapon. Folks forgot about things like brooms, ladders, and gardening tools. All of which could be used to smash a window without the perp getting so much as a nick.

After sweeping up as many of the big chunks as he could, he located a paper bag to use as a dustpan. He folded it over and swept up as much of the debris as he could. One thing that stood out about growing up a Firebrand was that each one knew how to be self-sufficient.

Had Adam developed a habit of depending on himself? To the extent he'd stopped letting others in?

Libby had told him she couldn't envision living her life on the ranch, waiting around for him to come home every day, no matter how much she loved him. And she'd used the word, *loved*. His heart had been wrecked and his judgment clearly had gone down with it when she showed up at his door, her cheeks stained with tears.

She'd told him how much she missed him and wished things could be different.

Still nursing a bruised ego, he'd taken her by the hand and led her inside. They didn't make it two steps in the door before her raincoat tumbled onto the floor and she stood there wearing nothing but a silk bra and panties.

Those details were etched into his mind, but the timing... The days ran together that time of year on a cattle ranch. He could rack his brain all day and still come up empty.

He walked over to the kitchen sink and wet a half dozen paper towels, a trick his mother had taught him to get all the shards. Growing up the oldest in a house of nine boys meant plenty of broken glass, be it someone dropping their drink or a ball through a window.

His childhood had been a good one despite all the fights that came with too much testosterone under one roof. Don't even get him started on the conflict that came with nine cousins, also boys, living on the same property.

Adam had claimed the fishing cabin for himself the day he'd turned eighteen, and there'd been no objections to him moving in on the last day of high school. His mother's only requirement was that he graduated. Sitting in a classroom for another four years sounded about as appealing as peeling wallpaper off walls with his thumbs, so he'd forgone the athletic scholarship waiting for him in favor of going straight into the family business. He'd taken two years' worth of online classes, enough to get an associate's degree in business.

"I'll take these samples in. It'll be anywhere from two to five days before I get the results from the lab," Lawler said.

This was going to be the longest few days of Adam's life.

"There any way to speed up the process?" Adam figured it was worth a shot to ask.

"I'm afraid not. I'll be calling in a favor to make a play, but I can't guarantee anything. I have no idea how backed up the lab is," Lawler explained.

"I'd appreciate a call the minute results come in," Adam said mostly for his own benefit. Lawler would call.

He nodded his reassurance.

"My deputy is filling out the report on the break-in

here," he said. "I have a few phone calls to make and a full inbox to attend to back at my office. I haven't been there at all since yesterday morning."

"Thank you for everything you're doing on the investigation," Adam said. Part of him wanted to ask to see Libby, to confirm with his own eyes she was gone. "How are Libby's parents taking the news?"

"They're shocked, of course," he admitted. "Said they hadn't seen her much since she moved to Austin. Needless to say, they weren't able to help much in the investigation. They couldn't say for sure who she'd been hanging around, who her friends were. She stopped posting on her social media page months ago."

"Could she have gotten herself in some type of trouble?" he asked.

"Time will tell," Lawler supplied. "When the two of you were together, did you get the impression she was mixed up with anything that might get her in a bad position?"

"No," he admitted. "But then, I didn't see her walking out on me when I asked her to be my wife either."

He'd misjudged the situation, thinking she was as happy as he'd been. Funny thing about it, though. Now that he'd spent time with Prudence, he didn't hold his relationship with Libby in as high a regard. Prudence was changing the kind of attraction he should feel with the person he wanted to spend his life with. Not that he was saying Prudence was *the one.* That ship had sailed when his chest had been split in two.

But if he was going to go head down that road again, it would be for someone like her.

The revelation caught him off guard. He chalked it up to his overwrought emotions over the Marshall dying coupled with the news he might be a father. *A father*, he repeated, trying it on for size.

He couldn't say it fit, but he would want a sweet girl like Angel if it was forced on him. An annoying little voice in the back of his head pointed out that he'd been natural with her so far. Was there an invisible bond between father and daughter?

Adam decided he wouldn't get too far ahead of himself. The paternity news could come out different. The chances Libby had gotten pregnant after having sex one time while using contraception had to be damn small. Except wasn't that how it always seemed to work out? When folks weren't trying or when it was the worst possible timing?

Rather than put too much emphasis on the thought, he tossed the paper bag remnant that was still in his hand. As he opened the trash, he saw something that caused his heart to thump wildly against his ribcage. A handwritten note with familiar writing.

Lawler extended his hand before leaving.

"Hold on a second, Sheriff. There's something in here you should take a look at," he said.

"Is it safe in here?" Prudence stood at the entrance to the kitchen with the baby in her arms.

Adam couldn't but think her question was loaded with the discovery. With his thumb and forefinger, he plucked the grocery list out of the trash. He shook the glass off before holding it up in the air.

"Is this yours?" he asked her.

Lawler's eyes widened as he got a close-up of the writing. He cleared his throat and took a step back, turning his full attention toward Prudence.

"What?" she asked, walking over to examine the specimen for herself. Her lips pursed together and a wrinkle creased her forehead. "That looks like my grocery list. Why?"

"I still have the sample in my SUV. Hold on," he said.

A mix of anger and disbelief rocked Adam to the core. He didn't want to accept what was plain as the nose on his face.

"What's going on, Adam?" Prudence crossed the room to get a closer look.

How could she not see it?

"I don't understand," she said. "What's happening here?"

"This doesn't look familiar to you at all?" He couldn't believe she would stand there and lie to him or pretend she didn't know. She couldn't use the excuse of not being able to remember with this one.

"Yes. I already said so. It's my grocery list," she said. "I just don't know what the big deal..."

Recognition seemed to dawn as Lawler re-entered through the back door. He held out the piece of paper from yesterday. The handwriting on the grocery list might be neater, but the letters were obviously written by the same person.

"What the hell, Prudence? Why is this your handwriting?"

11

"I-I-I...this can't be." Prudence shook her head, trying to find some way to clear out the fog and remember.

The look of betrayal in Adam's eyes nearly gutted her.

"I promise I didn't know that I wrote the note," she defended. Asking him to believe her when evidence said otherwise would take a leap of faith on his part. She could only hope he'd gotten to know her enough in the past twenty-four hours to realize she wouldn't try to pull the wool over his eyes.

But she did have a severe memory lapse. For three days, in fact.

"I need to find my cell," she said into the otherwise quiet room. She handed over the baby and dashed over to her laptop. "I should be able to find my cell using an app."

She broke the silence with the click-clack-clack of her fingers on the keyboard. How could she have written that note and not remembered?

The screen came to life and her work calendar immediately popped up.

"Oh no," she said. "I never leave this open."

"The perp might have checked to see where you would be next since you weren't home," Lawler offered.

"I thought I was off for a while but according to my schedule, I took a job starting tomorrow. I have to call my clients. There's no way I can work right now. Not with everything going on," she said.

"I'll send someone over to explain the situation," Lawler said.

Adam's silence was deafening.

"I need to call them personally." She realized that would be impossible without her phone. The walls suddenly felt like they were closing in around her and she couldn't breathe. Anxiety pressed against her chest like a boulder. She couldn't allow it to win.

Breathe, she reminded.

Slowly, she took in a deep breath and then exhaled for the same length of time. She could do this. She could get through this. This seemed like a good time to remind herself how far she'd come. She'd been through so much worse and survived.

"Don't you have a password to protect your laptop?" Adam finally asked, his voice a study in calm.

"Do you leave your keys in your truck when you run into the feed store?" she countered.

"Good point," he admitted.

"I live alone. Didn't think I'd need one," she said by way of explanation. "I need to send the Ramseys an e-mail. I'll let them know that I'm okay but a deputy will be stopping by. I don't want them to have something like this dropped on them out of the blue."

Lawler nodded as Adam walked into the adjacent living

room. What? Now he couldn't be in the same room with her?

As damning as the handwriting situation was, she had no doubt about her innocence. Didn't mean she could explain any of this, but she knew in her heart she could never hurt another person.

Did he doubt her?

Fingers dancing across the keyboard, she took in another deep breath. At least the computer located her cell.

"Here, we go," she said. "I found it."

She blew up the map and pinpointed the location. "That's my address. But there's no way it's here." Wouldn't she have seen it by now? Plus, her car wasn't parked out front and her purse was nowhere to be found." She glanced at the sheriff and then Adam. "Quick. Someone call me." She rattled off her number as the sheriff obliged.

Walking from room to room, she listened for her ringtones.

Nothing.

"Well, we know it has to be around here somewhere." Panic squeezed her chest. How could this be? How could her phone be right under their noses? "This won't help finding my car."

"I can help with that," Lawler said. "What's the make and model and license plate?"

She rattled them off and he immediately spelled them out on his radio along with a few acronyms she didn't understand.

"We'll see if anything turns up," Lawler said.

He had resources around the county. If her vehicle was ditched somewhere, maybe they could find it and that could give them another hint as to where she'd been.

Something had to have happened in the three lost days that would connect the dots. There had to be an explanation. Would she ever regain those memories and be able to explain? Having information locked inside her brain, inaccessible, was one of the most frustrating things she'd ever experienced.

"Maybe it's outside somewhere," Adam finally piped in. "The perp might have ditched it on his way out when we surprised him."

"You two check the perimeter. I'll nose around in here if it's okay with you, Prudence," Lawler said.

"Be my guest." She couldn't imagine he'd find anything inside her place. She'd already gone room to room, and nothing looked out of place. Another shiver raced down her back at the thought of someone being inside her home.

She followed Adam outside but headed in the opposite direction as him.

"Hey." He seemed to notice she wasn't behind him based on his hushed, irritated tone.

She rounded the corner to where he was standing, looking at her like she'd just stole the keys to his truck.

"You've been with me for the past eighteen hours, Adam," she said, not bothering to hide her frustration.

His expression was unreadable as he studied her.

"Have you made up your mind about my character yet?" She couldn't help but let off some steam with her comment. A growing part of her was proud of the bravado. The old Prudence would never have confronted anyone or demanded to know what they thought of her. The new one wanted to know where she stood.

"I'm doing my best here," he said by way of defense.

"Yeah? So am I. And, by the way, your best isn't good enough for me." There. She'd said it. She deserved to be around someone who believed in her.

Rather than stand there while moisture formed in her eyes, giving away just how emotional saying that to him was, she tucked her chin to her chest and circled back.

There were no footsteps behind her like her foolish heart wanted there to be.

His loss, she decided. She might not know why she'd scribbled his name on a piece of paper or tucked it inside the baby's blanket. Hell, she still didn't know why she had the child in the first place. But she knew *herself,* which was far more important at the moment. She would never harm another person. It just wasn't in her DNA. She could barely be rude to someone who cut her off in traffic.

And no matter how forthright she seemed to be becoming with her emotions, she didn't have a mean bone in her body. No one could tell her different. She wouldn't conspire against anyone or take a child away from her mother.

Prudence dropped onto her hands and knees to search inside the shrubbery. She poked around in bushes. Although, she should probably be searching the back of the house where the perp had come from when he left her house.

The creep must have been watching from somewhere in front of the house. She glanced up at the windows that looked onto the street. Again, the thought of someone setting up inside her house ready and waiting caused painful stabs in her chest.

A few rogue tears spilled out of her eyes, dropping onto the hard dirt.

Hurt filled her chest at the thought of Adam distrusting her so much, especially after feeling like he'd been her lifeline. Running her hand along the parched earth, she felt around.

When she found nothing, she sat back on her heels.

"Hey," Adam's voice startled her.

She gasped before bringing her hands up to take off her glasses and then wipe her eyes. No way was she going to let anyone see that she'd been crying. Technically, only a handful of drops fell but they were a few too many.

"Did you find anything?" she asked, not bothering to turn to look at him. She needed a minute to remember her frustration because making eye contact with him when she felt so vulnerable would be a mistake.

"No. I couldn't concentrate with you up here looking around on your own, so I thought I'd join you if that's okay with you." There was an emotion present in his voice that she recognized as guilt. He'd stopped short of apologizing, not that it would matter. If he didn't believe in her there was no use in being around each other.

"You can look anywhere you want. No one is going to stop you." The words came out a little sharper than she intended.

She had no plans to take them back, though.

ADAM DIDN'T KNOW what to think. His heart wanted to believe she had nothing to do with the case beyond showing up on his family's land with the baby. A Good Samaritan who'd stepped in to help a child in need.

How naïve would he be to go down that road again? One that led with feelings instead of logic. He'd been burned once and still felt the sting almost a year later. The baby, if she belonged to him, was a stark reminder of how quickly a relationship could go south and how much collateral damage could be done.

But, man, his heart wanted to go hook, line, and sinker into believing in Prudence.

He was so angry at hearing about Libby's senseless murder and the fact this child would be forced to grow up without her mother that he couldn't think straight. The whole situation was unfair to an innocent child.

Even if Angel wasn't his, he had half a mind to file a petition to adopt her. Libby couldn't possibly have believed in the father or she would have sent the child to him.

Those last words stuck in his thoughts. Maybe she had been.

Either way, he didn't like Prudence being out here exposed with no protection. The sheriff's SUV parked in front of the home might not detour the sonsofbitches who'd orchestrated a break-in. Don't even get him started on what they must've planned to do with her once she came home.

These creeps must have known she had the baby. It was the only explanation that made sense. Were they coming for Angel? What would they have done to Prudence? The same thing they'd done to Libby?

Didn't that thought send a shot of adrenaline racing through him?

More anger ping-ponged through him, seeking an outlet. Normally, a long day at the ranch worked out any and all frustrations. If a day of setting posts and repairing fences didn't knock the wind out of him, a good workout would.

Considering he had to help take care of Angel, those options weren't exactly on the table. Figuring out a non-physical way to deal with his emotions was about as fun as licking a bowl of toothpaste.

After searching for half an hour, Prudence stood up and announced, "I'm going around back now."

Since Adam had searched his side of the front yard with a fine-toothed comb, he joined her. Maybe he should just retrace the perp's footsteps. Adam imagined bolting out of the back door. The perp had to have seen Adam or been alerted by some person or persons parked out front.

The guy had been in a hurry. So, he'd bolted out the backdoor and cut east. Adam followed the trail. Prudence seemed to catch on when she joined him.

At the chain-link fence where the perp jumped over, metal glinted in the sunlight.

Prudence must have seen it around the same time because she made a beeline in the direction Adam was about to head. She dropped down and then came right back up with a cell phone in her hand.

"This is mine," she said, pressing her thumb onto the pad to bring the device to life.

It was too late to remind her the sheriff might have been able to lift a print and he couldn't blame her for going for it. He'd caught it himself too late to warn her.

"Is there anything out of the ordinary?" he asked as she studied the screen.

"No, but this makes me think they have my purse as well as access to my car." She issued a sharp sigh.

"Your wallet would have ID in it. Your address would be easy enough to lift from there," he said, grateful she was talking to him again.

"Did you find something?" Lawler came out the backdoor.

"Her cell," Adam supplied.

"Nothing looks off. I have security on my phone, so I doubt they got anything from it," she said.

"Most folks know we can track a cell phone down nowadays," Lawler said.

"Common knowledge," Adam agreed. "So, the perp was trying to bring law enforcement to Prudence's house? Why would they do that?"

Lawler studied the back door for a long moment. His gaze unfocused, like he went inside his head to find an answer or recall information. Maybe he was trying to put himself inside the perp's head.

He walked to the door and then did an about-face. He jogged over to the side of the house, mimicked seeing the two of them rounding the corner. Then, he raced over to the fence and faked a jump. He reached for the top of the fence and the cell tumbled out of his hand.

"Could have been an accident that he lost her phone," Lawler said after careful consideration.

"In the heat of the moment, the perp could have realized he dropped it but knew there was no time to hop back over the fence to retrieve it," Adam added.

"Could be." Prudence, who had been quiet up until then, made the same walk as Lawler. "Or, he could have ditched the phone because he realized we would be onto him now."

"Yep," Lawler confirmed. "That is certainly the next possibility I was going to focus on."

"Either way, it's still not safe for you to stay here tonight." Adam wasn't sure why he felt the need to remind her. "The offer to come to the main house still stands."

Whether he was ready to admit it or not, he needed her in so many more ways than one.

12

Time was getting away from Prudence. Angel would need another bottle soon and Adam needed time to get home, which was a solid hour drive from her place.

"I appreciate the offer. I'll have to think about it," she said. She hadn't made up her mind about going back with him just yet.

"Where else would you go?" It looked like Adam took a physical blow at hearing her words.

"There are plenty of places. In fact, there's a motel up next to the highway. Nothing wrong with going there for a few days until this whole mess gets sorted out." She looked to the sheriff. "Unless you need me to come to your office for questioning or something?"

The last part of her sentence was her asking if she was going to be under arrest.

"I don't see a reason for you to be uncomfortable at my office," he said. "If I need to get ahold of you, I have your cell now."

"What if the perp put some kind of tracking app on the cell?" Adam asked.

"It's possible," the sheriff stated. "Not likely since he tossed it in the yard. If he'd left it inside where she could easily see it, I might think otherwise."

Prudence stared at her phone with the same fear she would if she was staring at a bomb about to detonate. Icy fingers gripped her spine at the possibility someone could have planted an app on her phone and then ditched it in hopes she'd find it.

"You both said it was common knowledge that cell phones could be tracked," she said. "Leaving it on my table would be an even bigger giveaway."

Lawler nodded.

"If that's the case, I'd be more comfortable if it led them straight to you." She handed over the phone to the sheriff. "It occurs to me that without ID or a wallet, renting a room for a couple of nights will be impossible. So, if I can't say here, I might as well come back to the ranch."

The thought of being in the truck with Adam for a solid hour with no one else to talk to suddenly felt like a prison sentence.

"I better get to work patching up your back door," Adam said.

"I'll leave you to it," Lawler said. "I better get the tests turned into evidence."

Adam nodded, his expression unreadable as he handed over the baby to Prudence. "Do you have any supplies?"

"Hmm, good question. I don't have a garage to store anything in but I do have a hammer and nails," she said, not quite ready to warm up to him again. Once they got to the main house, rules could be set. It would take both of them to care for Angel. They could set a schedule. Take opposite feeding times while the other one slept. They barely had to be in the same room, except to make a handoff.

Besides, Prudence couldn't imagine walking away from Angel while the little girl's future was up in the air. She would do anything for that baby, even put up with Adam.

"I probably have something in the back of the truck to work with," he mumbled before heading toward his vehicle.

Apparently, he did. He returned with a board and a handful of supplies.

"This won't take but a minute," he said, going right to work.

The sheriff was long gone by that point. Adam would find out if he was a father in a matter of days when most folks had nine months to adjust to this kind of life-changing news to get ready for baby. He had a way with Angel. Prudence didn't want to use the word *natural,* but it was the closest that came to mind to describe seeing him feed and hold the baby. Angel had been swabbed too. She was too little to realize the implications if she came back a match to Adam's ex.

Again, her heart went out to the family. No matter what else happened, a woman had died.

Prudence made a mental note of everything she wanted to take with her. Definitely, her laptop. She didn't exactly need it, but she didn't want the perp returning and stealing it or busting it up. She walked through the bedroom, bouncing Angel and humming. Prudence couldn't remember the words to any lullabies but she knew the melodies.

A memory of her own mother singing to her at night before turning off the light struck. The sound was so sweet, it nearly brought Prudence to tears when she thought about it. Not sad tears, but tears of remembering. She'd forgotten so much about her parents and this was one of many buried memories.

Holding this sweetie in her arms reminded her what it was like to have a mother. Warmth washed over Prudence.

The stairs creaked but she didn't stop humming. Angel was awake, listening intently, like she was hearing a familiar sound. *Did your mother sing to you too?*

"I can take her whenever you're ready." Adam's masculine voice washed over Prudence. Not a good idea to have him inside her bedroom while she was still mad at him. The few sizzling-hot kisses they'd shared came to mind, causing a slow burn. Lucky for her, holding a baby quashed all thoughts of anything romantic happening between them.

"Okay," was all she managed to say through the crick in her throat. Her voice cracked on the one word.

She turned to face him and noted how his heft filled the doorframe as he leaned against the doorjamb. The man was sex on a stick gorgeous. Too bad he didn't trust her.

Actually, it was probably for the best when she thought about it as she walked over to him and then handed Angel over. She immediately turned her back and stepped away. Being close to that man was like standing in the sun. She pulled a travel suitcase out from underneath her bed and started packing.

"Did you decide on your next step?" Adam asked, his voice husky.

Prudence took a moment to consider her options. Going to the main house on the ranch really was the best option.

"I didn't mean to..." He stopped when his voice cracked. He cleared his throat before continuing, "I was a jerk earlier and that wasn't fair to you. I'm a work-in-progress on my anger and I never meant to direct it at you."

The sincerity in his voice touched her, but she wasn't ready to let him off the hook.

She spun around to face him and then leaned back on the bed.

"You either trust me or you don't," she said. "It's that simple."

"I trust you," he said without hesitation.

"Good, Adam. Because it hurt when you questioned me," she stated. "I realize I can't explain everything and there might be something else that comes up along with the investigation that is a shock. I may not know what happened for those three days I was taking that medication, but I do know that I would never hurt another human being, not intentionally."

"I believe you," he said like it was plain as the nose on his face.

"What changed your mind?" She needed to know the answer.

"I've seen you with Angel. There's no reason for you to take care of her. By all accounts, you don't want children of your own. At least, not at this point in your life. You could have handed her over and walked away. It wouldn't have made you heartless to get on with your life. But you didn't. You somehow ended up on our land, looking for me. The look of determination to protect that little girl at all costs is extraordinary, Prudence." He glanced down at Angel and then his gaze found hers. "You have no ties to a child you'd give your life for. It takes a special person to be willing to put herself in harm's way for another human being, especially one so helpless."

Her heart stirred at hearing his words, but she couldn't

allow herself to go there with him. Clearly, he had the power to shatter her. So, she would keep a healthy emotional distance while she made sure Angel was well cared for until her father was found or Libby's family members came forward.

"Thank you for the kind words," she said with a small smile. "We should probably head out of here if we're going to make it the main house before she's ready for another feeding."

Shame, she thought about her growing feelings for Adam. He was the first person in a very long time she had a real connection with...one that would set the tone for future expectations. And that bar was high.

ADAM SAID his piece and meant it. The wall he felt come up between them hurt like hell, but he deserved it.

Her handwriting might be a match to the note found in the blanket, but what did it mean exactly? He was beginning to set aside his anger and think logically again. There could be a number of explanations, not the least of which was that she'd written his name down so she wouldn't forget it.

Once they got to his place, he'd see if he could find a picture of Libby to share. He'd deleted them after she hurt him. There might be one somewhere if he searched hard enough. Maybe seeing her face would jar Prudence's memory. The two of them together was a strange thought at best. Stranger coincidences had happened.

He also thought about Libby's family. Why wouldn't they know she was pregnant? Why would Libby keep a grandchild from them? A relationship with him was one thing and had been a red flag, to be honest. He'd been too love-sick to take it seriously at the time but it had hit his radar.

Unlike with Prudence where there were question marks but no red flags.

There was no use dwelling on it, though. He'd nipped that in bud before it could get off the ground with his attitude earlier. A wall had come up so high in between them there'd be no tearing it down.

Shame, he thought.

Now, that Libby's family knew she'd had a kid, would they come after Angel? He tightened his arms around the little girl who was staring up at him with the most innocent pair of eyes. To be able to look at the world like that again, through the eyes of a child.

"Ready?" Prudence stood five feet away from him with her overnight bag in hand.

He'd been too lost in thought to notice.

With the back window boarded up, there wasn't much else to do at Prudence's house. "We need to stop off and pick up a few supplies."

"I noticed she's getting low on diapers and formula," Prudence agreed as she led them downstairs. "I'll just use the spare key to lock up."

She retrieved it along with her laptop before heading to the truck and helping secure Angel in the car seat.

They were back on the road a solid ten minutes before either of them spoke a word.

"If Libby withheld Angel from her parents, she must've had a good reason," he finally said. One he intended to figure out.

"You never met them?" Shock widened her eyes when she glanced over at him.

He immediately returned his gaze to the road. "No."

"Oh," was all she said by way of response. Then came, "Doesn't seem like she was close to her family if she didn't introduce them to a man she almost married."

"Anytime the subject of her folks came up, she got quiet. I assumed she had her reasons and would tell me once we got engaged. Normally, that's the time when families get involved, if not during the dating process," he said.

"I always assumed Firebrands were close-knit," she admitted.

"Some of us are. Between eight brothers and nine cousins there's always a fight going on and plenty of others to connect with. I'm probably closest to my brother Brax, who you already met."

"Which one of you is the oldest?" she asked.

"Me, on my side of the family. My cousin Kellan on the other side. He's older than me by six months, but you'd think he had ten years on me by the way he thinks he's in charge," Adam admitted with a little more ire than intended. His anger management was a work in progress and thinking about his cousin fired him up. "I've been cutting him slack since his divorce, but our grandfather's property division might stir the pot."

Prudence sat there, looking out the window for the rest of the hour and fifteen-minute drive home. She stayed in the truck with Angel during the stop off.

Being in a vehicle knocked the kiddo out. Good to know, he thought, figuring he would need to keep tabs on all the tricks should she turn out to be his child. He needed as much in his arsenal as he could find because there'd come a time when Prudence would walk out and go back to her normal life and he'd be left to care for his child on his own.

Whoa there, Firebrand. Way to get ahead of the situation.

One hour at a time was how he would take things from

now on. Trying to look ahead would make his head explode. He didn't need to get used to the idea that Angel might be his. There was no reason to get attached and then set himself up for disappointment if paternity proved otherwise.

He pulled up to the main house and saw Brax's truck parked out front.

Adam parked next to his brother. He moved around the front of the truck too slow to open the door for Prudence, which he considered common courtesy.

"I have an idea," she said, snapping the car seat from its base, effectively turning it into a carrier. "We won't have to constantly hold her and she might be more comfortable napping in here."

Prudence had a point. The child's whole world had been turned upside-down. He had no idea if she had an inkling of what was going on around her, but his heart broke at the only thing they knew for certain; her mother was dead.

"Hey." Brax met the trio at the door. He immediately offered to take Prudence's bag.

"Thank you," she said.

Adam liked the fact his favorite brother got along with Prudence. There seemed to be a mutual kinship between them that tugged at his heartstrings. Not that he needed to go down that road with Prudence, where she got along with his family.

After bags were set down and the baby was secured on a chair wedging it against the table for security purposes, Brax motioned for Adam and Prudence to move to the island. Each took a seat as Brax paced on the opposite side.

"What's going on?" Adam asked, figuring this had to have something to do with the Marshall.

"He did it." Brax raked a hand through his hair. "He split the ranch from the mineral rights."

The news was the equivalent of a hot poker against Adam's chest. The worst was most definitely yet to come and the family might never recover.

"All hell is about to break loose," Adam agreed.

"Why is that such a bad thing?" Prudence's question caught Adam off guard. He assumed it was common knowledge to everyone who lived around cattle ranches. But why would everyone know?

"Our father and uncle were given the wrong names," Brax said under his breath. "They should have been called Cain and Abel."

Adam would laugh if it wasn't true. Prudence nodded.

"Do you know who got what?" Adam's worst fear would be losing the cattle ranch to his uncle and cousins. They'd boot him off the land just to spite him even though his uncle didn't care two cents about cattle or ranching. He was only in the family business for the money.

"Dad got the cattle and the land," Brax stated.

"Which means they got the mineral rights," Adam deduced. He turned to Prudence, very aware of the chemistry pinging between them while sitting so close, and explained, "The reason this is gas on a fire is that our uncle can't drill without the land owner's permission. And the real money in a ranch is with mineral rights."

"Sounds like your grandfather had a wicked sense of humor," she mused.

"You're not wrong," Adam said. "It would just like the Marshall to try to force those two to stand on common ground."

"He had to know that Dad would never sell the ranch," Brax chimed in.

"But he could kick Uncle Keif and his family off," Adam said. Keifer Firebrand wouldn't stand for it.

"The Marshall deeded their homes to them," Brax said.

"Then, they can bulldoze their houses and drill there," Adam quipped. He shouldn't let emotions get the best of him. In fact, sitting close to Prudence was a reminder of the damage he could cause if he did.

He wouldn't make the same mistake twice.

"Check that," he said. "Maybe we can talk to Dad and see if he's willing to compromise."

Brax laughed.

"You clearly weren't here to witness the fireworks," he said. "Lines have already been drawn. Dad threatened to kick Uncle Keif off the land. It's the reason we know he can't."

"I can only imagine the blowout that must've caused." Adam shook his head. His precious land was safe but family relationships just got a whole lot messier.

"Uncle Keif is threatening to contest the will," Brax said.

"His hands are the most tied because he can't do what he wants and there's a boatload of money in mineral rights." Adam wasn't surprised at his uncle's knee-jerk reaction. "It won't do any good to contest the will. If I know the Marshall, that thing will be ironclad."

"There's a catch," Brax said. "One that I don't think any of us expected."

Well, that news got Adam's attention.

"If the Marshall's sons can't come to an agreement before all their sons are married, they lose everything. The inheritance goes directly to us and both land and mineral rights are equally split," Brax said.

Adam almost laughed out loud.

"Considering there's eighteen of us and not one of us is currently married, I doubt that's a big threat," he said. It was just like the Marshall to do something like that. Adam had no plans to wed after Libby. Now that he might be a father, he'd be too busy caring for an infant to date for the foreseeable future. The annoying voice in the back of his mind picked that moment to point out his chemistry with Prudence and how incredible she was with baby Angel.

"I'd agree with that assessment except that our dad and uncle can dig their heels in when they really want to. Being stubborn seems to be part of the Firebrand DNA," Brax stated.

Prudence didn't hold back a grin.

"I'm sure Kellan is blowing a gasket." Adam smirked. He couldn't help himself.

Brax chuckled. "Let's just say he's not shy with his opinion."

The baby started fussing in the next room. Adam checked the clock. Eight p.m. on the dot.

"I'll take care of her and let the two of you finish talking family business." Prudence seemed eager to leave the room. He shouldn't take it personally, and yet he did.

Sucking in his pride, he leaned forward, clasping his hands together on the island.

Brax stared at Adam for a long moment, and it looked like he was holding back.

Rather than goad his brother on, Adam changed the subject. "Speaking of food. Have you eaten yet?"

"Me? No. I wanted to fill you in the minute you got home," Brax said. "I put security on notice to let me know the minute you pulled up to the front gate."

Adam crossed over to the fridge, pulled out a sealed container of meatloaf with a side of mashed potatoes and string beans. Miss Olive must have anticipated company following the Marshall's death. A normal family might gather at the main house. But then, Firebrands had never been considered typical.

"Thanks for coming over to let me know what was going on," Adam said.

"It's what brothers are for." Brax didn't miss a beat, but there was much more to their relationship than blood ties.

"Not every brother feels the same," Adam said. He could add a few of his cousins to that list as well.

"Anything I should know about what's going on with..." Brax motioned toward the adjacent room.

"Nothing to say there." Adam wasn't ready to define his relationship with Prudence or defend it to anyone either. For now, he wasn't ready to talk about the current situation with Angel. Brax would be the first to know when Adam was.

He heated three plates as Brax set the table. By the time Prudence joined them, dinner was ready to go.

She walked into the room, and then froze when her gaze landed on the table nicely set for three. "Wow. I'm impressed."

"The least I can do is feed you," Adam said.

Brax shot a look but thankfully kept his lips locked.

"This smells amazing," she said, fists resting on her hips.

"I'm glad to hear it. I can't take credit for cooking. All I did was throw a couple of plates in the microwave," he said, holding out a hand like he was presenting a new car. "Shall we dig in?"

Prudence didn't waste time, walking over and taking the seat being offered. She made quick work of the meatloaf and potatoes, but mostly pushed around the green beans with her fork.

SEEING Adam and Brax's interactions reminded Prudence of her sister. Shayla had been three years older and a whole lot sassier. She was all flash and personality in the best possible way, forever twelve years old in Prudence's mind.

The murderer who'd taken her family away had done her a small favor in blindfolding her while he performed the deed. This way, she didn't have images replaying in her mind over and over again, and she'd learned to shut off her imagination when it came to what might have happened. The neighbor had shielded Prudence from the horror of seeing what had happened. Knowing had been bad enough.

She listened as Adam and Brax talked about their family drama. If not for her aunt and uncle, she would feel very alone in the world. She was thankful she had them, at least.

The idea of being part of a big family had never appealed to her before. Except being in this kitchen, she could almost smell the fresh cookies around the holidays. She imagined pies and more food than anyone could eat. Somehow with all the guys on this ranch, she doubted there would ever be a leftover no matter how much food was placed out on the island or the kitchen table.

She secretly liked the fact they'd eaten in the kitchen over the formal dining room she'd walked past earlier. It was nice in there, don't get her wrong, but there was something cozy in this room. It was warm and informal, like she imagined a family meal should be.

Growing up, she'd eaten most meals from a TV tray while watching nighttime soap operas with her relatives. They'd been kind people. And yet, she missed her parents and sister. Her mother's singing.

The memory came back full force earlier in the bedroom with Angel.

"I better get going," Brax finally said after dessert and coffee. He turned to Prudence. "It's nice seeing you again."

"I feel the same," she admitted, and it was true. She might not want to get attached to Adam or his family, but they were intelligent and warm. It would be impossible to completely turn off her affection for them. Of course, she'd only met two of his brothers. Fallon had always been nice to her, even when others walked right past. There must be something about the Firebrand bloodline that made them kind to strangers.

Despite Adam not being as close with the others, she'd never heard a bad word about anyone in the family. Then again, she would be last to hear gossip. Keeping to herself had some advantages. Plus, she interacted with her clients on an almost weekly basis.

Why did her old life seem empty to her now?

A week ago she'd been more than happy with her small existence. She had the occasional date when she went into Austin, but no one who blew her hair back. She started to say, "Like Adam," but stopped herself.

She enjoyed the anonymity of living in town and blending in. Everyone left her alone and she did her own thing. Suddenly, her life sounded lonely, which was strange because it was exactly what she'd built.

Being with Adam had her realizing there was so much more out there. Interesting conversation. Someone who made her feel incredibly beautiful without ever saying the words. Someone who made her feel safe even though he also made her feel things she'd never experienced. Like chemistry beyond her wildest imagination. And the pull of the hottest kisses that would turn into the most mind-blowing sex she would ever have.

She stopped herself right there. The last things she needed to be thinking about were sizzling kisses and blazing inferno sex.

"How's the little girl?" Brax asked, motioning toward the adjacent room.

Interesting that Adam hadn't told his brother and best friend that she might be related to him.

"Doing all right. Might have bad news on the mother," Adam said.

"That's a shame." Brax shook his head. The news clearly affected him.

"We're waiting on word from the sheriff to figure out the next moves," Adam informed. "But she'll be here for the time being."

"Good of you both to step in like this," Brax said. "I'll cover for you on the ranch. Take all the time you need."

"I appreciate it," Adam said. Their affection for each other sent warmth spiraling through her.

It wasn't the first time she'd gotten all warm and fuzzy while witnessing a family moment. The rare time she went to the park and saw a father teaching his son or daughter how to ride a bike or watched siblings holding hands practically gutted her. She'd teared up at a commercial more than once. Don't even get her started on movies. She carefully curated those to avoid touching family moments. Why torture herself?

Time made it easier and she truly was grateful to have an aunt and uncle willing to step in. She might not have been close with them, but that didn't stop her appreciation for what they'd done.

Brax excused himself and took off down the hallway toward the front door.

"Mind if I get some fresh air?" Prudence asked, nodding toward the back.

"Go right ahead," Adam said, as he bit back a yawn.

"Are there any dogs I need to worry about back there?" she asked.

"Nothing to worry about. Most of the animals prefer to stick around the barns this time of year. If you walk that far, you might run into a dog or two. All are used to folks and friendly," he said. "But you probably won't see any."

She must've frowned because he asked, "Can I ask why you don't have a pet? It's obvious you care about them."

"Too much commitment," she said before heading toward the back door.

She glanced back at the house and more of those Normal Rockwall images crept in. A fireplace lit on a cold night. Christmas decorations everywhere during the holidays. People laughing and the hum of chatter drifting outside.

Was a life like that possible for her?

She'd never once allowed herself to imagine it. Why was that? Could she call her aunt and uncle and ask them what was broken inside her? Why she didn't grow up dreaming of having a family of her own or cut out pictures of her future wedding dress?

Why couldn't she see herself with a husband and kids?

A little voice in the back of her mind added, *until Adam.* But she quieted it down before it could get going. Of course, she would feel a certain pull toward the man who'd rescued her in the trees out on ranch property. Of course, she would fall for his daughter. Angel was more description than name. The little girl had wormed her way in Prudence's heart from the minute she could remember looking down at her.

Prudence could feel the spark between her and Adam. She'd have to be crazy not to. But it didn't mean anything. Besides, she had a feeling his life was about to be turned upside-down when the paternity news came in.

He might not be ready to admit it yet, but the likelihood he was Angel's father was high.

Right now, she would set all those thoughts aside and let the warm breeze tickle her face. This place had a magic of its own. The lawn was something out of a magazine with a large oak tree complete with tire swing off to one side. There was a dotting of trees to shade the house, no doubt planted a hundred years ago when the home was built. It had clearly been updated since then. The trees had stretched toward the sky before reaching toward each other to create a shield over the magnificent two-story.

Stretching her legs felt good after being in the truck for a more than two hours round trip. She'd never been one for long car rides. She extended her arms out to her sides, then clasped her fingers and brought her hands up over her head.

Holding the baby for hours on end might be satisfying, but it was hard on the body. She dropped her arms to her sides and then shook out her hands, needing to get the blood flowing again.

After a couple of laps around the house, she entered the house through the same door she used earlier.

"She just walked inside." Adam stood at the island with his cell phone on speaker as he locked gazes with her.

Alarm bells sounded in her mind and an ominous feeling settled over her. She recognized the tone.

"What?" she mouthed to him.

He motioned for her to stand next to him. She walked to the opposite side of the island and planted herself by placing her palms down, arms spread out.

"I'm here," she said.

"Good. I'd like for both of you to hear this together." The voice was easily recognizable as Lawler's. There was a buzz in the background. His radio squawked and she heard something that sounded like road noise.

Her chest squeezed.

"We're listening," Adam said with a weary look that said he didn't want to hear more bad news any more than she did. They'd had enough for one day, more like a lifetime when she really thought about it.

"Deputy Smithfield stopped by to talk to your clients a few minutes ago." Lawler paused just like he'd done the last time he'd delivered bad news.

"What did they say? Were they understanding?" Prudence hated letting her clients down, and yet there wasn't much that could be done.

"They're deceased," Lawler said with a reverence normally reserved for church service on Sunday.

Prudence's stomach roiled.

14

"I'm going to be sick."

Adam couldn't get around the island fast enough. Prudence spun around in time to empty the contents of her stomach into the sink. With her background, this ordeal must be bringing up all kinds of horrific memories. And, if not memories, then emotions.

He wet a paper towel as she rinsed out her mouth. With the faucet sprayer, he hosed down the bile as she took the offering from him and pressed the cool rag to her forehead.

Lawler waited patiently on the line as Prudence gathered herself.

"I'm sorry," she mumbled.

"Hey," he said, "Don't ever apologize for having feelings. Okay?"

She pushed her hair off her face, tucking a loose tendril behind her ear. Her cheeks flushed but he couldn't tell if she was embarrassed or nauseous again.

"Mind if I grab a glass of water?" she asked.

He grabbed a bottle of water from the fridge. She took the offering and pressed it against her cheek, then her neck.

At least the baby was sleeping in the next room.

"Let me know when you're ready to continue," Adam said to Prudence. "Or, I can take it from here."

"Thanks, but I need to hear this," she said, walking back to the island. "Please, keep going."

"Are you sure?" Lawler's tone told Adam the story was about to get worse. Much more so.

"I can handle it. I was just caught off guard before," Prudence said, opening the top of the bottle before taking a long drink.

"It never gets easier to hear something like this," Lawler admitted. "I've been on the job as sheriff for a decade now and I can attest to the fact."

"I can imagine," she said, bringing her free hand up to cover her heart. "I'm ready now."

"The scene is set up to look like a murder-suicide," Lawler continued.

"What do you mean by 'set up'?" Adam clued in immediately to the word choice.

"Exactly that. I think it's been arranged to throw us off track. The connection between cases is Prudence and the baby," Lawler said.

"Why do you think that?" Prudence asked, referring to the set up.

"There's a suicide note." Lawler hemmed and hawed on this next part. He didn't seem too eager to share what it said.

"Who wrote it?" Prudence asked.

"Allegedly, Mrs. Ramsey," he supplied.

"I'm guessing she explained why she killed her husband," Prudence continued after taking another sip of water.

"According to the note, he was having an affair," Lawler

said. "In the times you were around them, did they seem like a happy couple to you?"

Prudence's forehead creased. "Yes. Most people who went on vacation together were pretty excited to see me so they could leave and spend some time together. They weren't any different."

"So, you never witnessed any arguments between the two of them?" he continued.

"No. To be fair, I was never around the couple. I watch their dog. Miss Peabody is their bichon. Hutch is their lab. He's all over the place with his energy but make no mistake about it, Miss Peabody is the one in charge. Why?" she asked.

"Because according to this note, Mrs. Ramsey killed her husband and named his mistress, saying she had to kill her too." Lawler got real quiet. "The mistress named in the note is you."

Adam didn't believe it for one minute.

PRUDENCE BLINKED A FEW TIMES, trying to let Lawler's statement sink in. She knew she wasn't having an affair with Mr. Ramsey or anyone else for that matter. At the present time, her heart wanted to be with the impossible man in the room with her, his hand on her lower back.

She needed to know what Lawler thought.

"You don't be—"

"No," he cut in before she had time to finish. It was the obvious question to ask. "The note references you as already dead."

She tried not to vomit again as bile climbed up her throat, burning a trail to her mouth.

Adam's thumb drew circles at the small of her back and brought a surprising amount of comfort with his touch. She couldn't think about the senseless loss of two lives and still keep a clear mind. With great effort, she had to put those emotions aside—emotions that threatened to pull her under and trigger feelings from her traumatic past.

Years of therapy from her youth kicked in, and she remembered to focus on something real, something that kept her in the present and aware of being inside her own body. Like the light, reassuring touch on her back. She used Adam's hand to ground her. Mr. and Mrs. Ramsey deserved justice.

"Let me see if I have this right. Someone broke into the Ramsey home with the intention of killing them and setting the scene to look like a murder-suicide. Prudence was to be...what...ambushed?...when she showed up at six o'clock in the morning to care for their pets where she would also be killed and 'arranged' to fit," Adam surmised.

"The note was already written, so, that's exactly the way this looks," Lawler stated.

"In the hopes of gaining what?" Prudence could feel the blood rush out of her face. Dizziness set in but she had no plans to let it take over. *Breathe.* She looked at her hands that were planted against the island and focused on the feel of the granite beneath her fingers.

And then it dawned on her.

"The baby," came out in a whisper.

"Someone wants this angel pretty badly," Lawler suggested.

"Is there any way to speed up the paternity test based on this new information? I can't help but think this would have to settle down if I can claim her as mine legally," Adam said.

"You know I'm doing my best there," Lawler said in his usual calm tone.

Prudence had no idea how he did it. A job like his would undo her. There was no way she would want a front-row seat to people's worst days. She was grateful for lawmen like him. The detective who'd taken her to child protective services had been a godsend. She couldn't remember his name anymore or the details of his face. All she could recall was a dark-haired man in a suit with a kind, steady voice and a teddy bear taking her to a foster family until her next of kin could be notified and cleared through the courts to come pick her up. The same detective had been present when her aunt and uncle pulled up in their small pickup. She'd sat in the middle and her aunt held her hand the entire drive to their home.

No words had been spoken, or, if they had, she couldn't say what they were. All she remembered clearly was clinging to that teddy bear like it was her lifeline.

"Elizabeth's parents made an appointment to come to my office at seven a.m. tomorrow to give statements before he goes into work. You're welcome to come down and hear what they have to say," Lawler said. "I can arrange for you to be in a sound-proof room with a two-way mirror."

"I'd like that very much," Adam immediately piped in.

"Stop by half hour before the meeting. Say, six-thirty," Lawler said.

"What's going to happen to Miss Peabody and Hutch?" Prudence couldn't stand the thought of the dogs ending up in a shelter after what they'd been through.

"They're with animal control," Lawler said.

Prudence shot a desperate glance at Adam. He seemed to immediately pick up on the meaning.

"Any chance they can be released into our custody?" he asked.

"I can have that arranged," Lawler said.

"Is it possible to pick them up now? They must be so scared." Prudence balled her fists. She flexed and released her fingers a few times trying to work off some of the tension.

The baby stirred in the adjacent room, working up to a cry.

Adam caught her gaze, as though making sure it was okay to step away and attend to Angel.

Prudence nodded, missing his touch the minute the pressure on the small of her back changed.

"I can do one better than that," Lawler said. "Animal control can swing them by on their way to the shelter. It'll ease their burden anyway."

The first glimmer of hope lit inside Prudence. She loved those dogs, and they didn't deserve what was happening. Neither did their owners and she felt helpless to do anything there. They were good people who should be finishing up packing for a vacation they'd planned and looked forward to for weeks, if not months. A rogue tear escaped as anger welled up inside her. She couldn't afford more than one.

"Thank you, Sheriff."

"It's the least I can do," he said quietly. "I'll be in touch if there's any additional news. In the meantime, it's probably a good idea to sit tight at the ranch."

She understood the implication. There was security at Firebrand unlike anything she'd ever seen. She would be safe there.

"Will do," she said as Adam joined her with a teary-eyed

Angel in his arms. She was sucking on her binky like there was no tomorrow. Did she have a bad dream? A memory?

Prudence had no idea what a newborn was capable of. But she was one hundred percent certain Angel was special.

Lawler ended the call.

"I'm sorry about your clients," Adam said.

"Someone must want that little girl awfully bad to go to this much trouble to get her back," Prudence observed.

"She leaves this ranch over my dead body," Adam stated. His look of determination said he would back those words up in a heartbeat.

"What do you think we should do with her in the morning?" Prudence didn't think it was safe to take her along to the sheriff's office and she needed to hear what Libby's parents had to say. Considering her life hung in the balance until this investigation was over, she figured she had a right to follow it along.

"Good question." And then the answer seemed to dawn on him. "How would you like to meet my mother?"

"Tonight?" She glanced down at her jogging suit as panic engulfed her. "Like this?"

"You'd be beautiful in a paper bag," he said without hesitation. Did he mean it? "But if you'd rather not, the house is huge. You can go upstairs and relax. I'll call when she's gone."

"It's getting late and animal control will be dropping off Hutch and Miss Peabody soon. I'd rather stay downstairs and keep watch for them," she rationalized. Besides, it wasn't like she was meeting his family in a formal sense. The two weren't even dating so her need to make a good impression had to take a backseat.

"I'll ask her to come over." He managed to balance the baby and make a call. His skills at handling Angel were improving by the minute. If she turned out to be his child, he was going to make one helluva father. "Make yourself comfortable."

"I might sit out front. It's a beautiful night," she said, wanting to be as far away from Adam and his family as possible. Her heart practically melted every time she saw him holding the baby.

"Suit yourself. My mom is a decent person, though. She's nothing like my father. You might actually like her if...never mind," he seemed to catch himself. "Looking at the stars at night is one of the main reasons I never felt a need to leave this ranch and is a big part of why this land, Texas, will always be a part of my soul. You always hear people talking about stopping to smell the roses when all they really have to do is walk outside in the evening and look up."

That was about the most beautiful thing she'd heard today.

Heading toward the front door, she heard his voice as he made the call to his mother. The tender way in which he spoke hit her square in the chest.

Out on the front porch, she sat down and hugged her knees. There was a slight chill in the air and a couple of clouds dotting in the sky. The promise of rain hung in the air. They needed it. The ground was so parched cracks were fracturing the earth.

Prudence had no idea how long she sat there in silence before the all-white animal services van pulled up. An older gentleman wearing all khaki-colored clothing exited the driver's side.

"Evening, ma'am. Mr. Firebrand said I'd find you here on the porch." He looked to be in his late fifties, early sixties. He was short by Texas standards, so probably five-feet-nine-inches. He had a ready smile, horse teeth, and a soft, round middle that looked like it might burst out of his shirt and pants in the same manner as a Pillsbury cinnamon roll can.

"Beautiful night," she said, liking small talk as opposed to the heavy conversations she had been having all day.

"Wish it would hurry up and rain already," he said, extending his hand. "Name's Randy, by the way."

She met him halfway, introduced herself, and took the offering. He had a firm shake.

"We sure need it," she agreed.

"Yep," he said before rounding to the side of the van and pulling out a set of keys.

She hated the thought of her buddies being locked up. She'd been sitting for Hutch and Miss Peabody since they were pups, so five and six years now respectively. The thought of them being broken up and adopted out to different households wasn't something she could handle.

Granted, her life was not built for keeping them permanently. Like everything in life, she would figure it out. There was no way she was letting these sweethearts suffer any more than they already had.

Randy let Hutch out first. The black lab came bolting out of the enclosure and straight toward her. He jumped on her, knocking her back a step.

"Whoa there, Hutch." She didn't bother telling him to calm down. He wouldn't be able to on a good day, let alone on what had to be his worst, even if he didn't fully understand what was happening. "Good boy."

He ran a few circles around the van and she figured he needed to stretch his legs.

Miss Peabody was much easier. The bichon shook like a leaf in a windstorm as Randy unlocked her enclosure. Her relief was palpable when she saw Prudence. She immediately took the dog from Randy.

"The sheriff asked me to drop off their leashes, food, and bowls," Randy stated, lumbering over to the back of his van. He unlocked another 'cell' and produced the items.

"Do you mind putting them on the porch for me?" She had her hands full soothing a distraught Miss Peabody.

"Not at all." Randy was strong as an ox. Hutch's food came in a fifty-pound bag and there were two of them, only one partially empty. Miss Peabody's came in the form of cans, so he set the medium-sized box next to the bags.

She whistled for Hutch and he came gunning for her. The only command the dog knew was, *sit.* So, she used it and he immediately planted his backside down before bowling her over.

"Good boy, Hutch," she said.

"Looks like you got this under control," Randy said with a smile. "I best be going."

"Thank you for bringing these guys here and all their stuff." Hutch's favorite toy was among the leashes.

She walked next to him as Randy waved, and then drove off.

Prudence had faced a lot today. Could she handle the woman inside the house?

15

Adam stood at the backdoor, watching as his mother walked toward the house. He was still trying to decide how much he should tell her about Angel and Prudence as he saw her cross the yard.

No answers came to him by the time she greeted him as he held the door open for her. She was short, barely five-feet-two-inches and had the blackest hair of anyone he'd ever seen, always piled on top of her head in a messy knot. Her Italian heritage shined through in her eyes, her cooking, and her warm personality even though she'd been born in America, just like her mother before her.

"Hey, Mom," he said by way of greeting.

Those deep brown eyes of hers skimmed him, like she was trying to figure out and prepare for just about anything. He didn't call her nearly enough. And he never called her at night. She'd be asleep in another half hour and most anything he ever had to say to her could wait until meatball dinner on Sundays, not that he always attended. Being in the same room with his father for too long was a problem.

"Everything okay, Adam?" She studied his face.

Angel was sleeping in her carrier, having just downed a bottle.

"Come on into the kitchen where we can talk," he said.

Her forehead wrinkled with concern as she passed by him. She moved toward the table and then froze. He recognized it as the instant she saw Angel.

"Who is this?" she whispered.

Since he still hadn't figured out how to explain who Angel was and why she belonged on the ranch with him, he decided to sidestep the question.

"How are your babysitting skills?" he asked.

The look he got for redirecting the conversation caught him off guard. He'd seen his mother so angry he thought her head might explode, though she never uttered a word in frustration. He'd seen her cry tears of joy. This was different.

"Good enough to keep the nine of you alive," she pointed out.

"That's why I called. I figure you're nine for nine, and I need someone to watch this little girl in the morning while I visit the sheriff's office," he stated, hoping she would let it go at that.

"So, you're helping out Sheriff Lawler by keeping her here?" his mother asked.

"Yes." It was the truth.

"And you can't go into the reasons behind it right now?" she asked.

"It's better if I don't." Again, he wasn't lying. Adam had been brought up to be honest. Honor was everything for a rancher.

She nodded before walking over to take a peek into the carrier. "A girl?"

"That's right," he said. His mother had made no secret about wishing to take home at least one pink blanket instead of nine blue. Her close friends and acquaintances knew she was the 'go to' if they needed a babysitter for their daughter. She'd loved her boys, though. Don't get him wrong. But a girl put a twinkle in his mother's eyes that neither Adam nor any of his brothers ever had.

"What time should I be here?" she asked. Her face lit up as she watched the sleeping angel.

"I have to leave around five-forty-five," he said. His mother kept rancher hours so she would be awake for a full hour and forty-five minutes at that point.

"Okay." She practically beamed at the baby and it gave him a little more confidence in sharing the news following the paternity test if Angel turned out to be his.

"One more thing, and this is a big ask," he said.

His mother took in a deep breath like she was fortifying herself.

"Keep this between us for now," he said.

Her eyes widened.

He put his hands up, palms out, in the surrender position. "The fewer people who know she's here, the better. That's all I'm saying."

"I never keep secrets from your father," she said. "What will I tell him is the reason I have to be here so early?"

"Do you have to say anything?" he asked.

"Heaven help me." She made the sign of the cross.

"If he asks, I wouldn't expect you to lie," he said. "Does he know where you are twenty-four/seven?"

She stood there for a long moment and he wasn't certain which way she was leaning.

"I guess not. If I came here to the main house, he might assume that I'm starting the process of going through his father's things," she reasoned.

"There's another purpose to stop by and I have no problem if you tell the world about—"

As if on cue, the click-click-click sound of toenails on tile echoed from down the hallway. The sound was a bullet train coming at them.

"Hutch," Prudence called out. Her voice lit campfires inside him. She was all blue skies and endless summer days.

A black lab came bolting into the kitchen. The minute he saw Adam, he put the brakes on. He couldn't gain traction, so he basically skidded across the room unable to stop until he plunked into the wall.

His back legs got out from underneath him and he struggled to pull it together again.

"Sit!" came the command from the hallway.

The dog complied.

Adam was impressed. His mother seemed shocked. Her hand immediately went out to block the dog from getting anywhere near the carrier. He'd never seen his mother move so fast.

Adam chalked it up to a mother's instincts.

She wedged her body in front of the baby and his chest tightened with pride. If Angel turned out to be his...

No sense going there at this point. He'd know soon enough, and he didn't need any expectations on the results either way. The situation was complicated enough without adding to it.

Prudence jogged into the room, carrying a little white puffball in her arms and issuing an apology. She froze the minute her gaze landed on Adam's mother.

"Mother, I'd like to introduce you to my friend Prudence," Adam said.

Out of the corner of his eye, he caught his mother eyeing

Prudence up and down. Was she checking for signs that this was the little girl's mother?

"Pleased to meet you," his mother said.

"It's such a pleasure. I was in the same grade as Fallon in school and I've heard so much about your family that I feel like I already know you," Prudence said, much to his mother's delight.

"If anyone asks where you're going tomorrow, you could always use the excuse of dog sitting," Adam suggested.

"I'm very impressed, by the way," his mother said to Prudence. "I've never been able to get a dog to listen to me like that."

"It comes with the territory for me." Prudence's cheeks flushed at the compliment and it made her look even more beautiful. "I own a pet sitting company and it's the one thing I work on before I accept a new client. If I can't get the dog to sit from anywhere in the room or no matter what else he or she is doing, I don't want to be responsible for them."

"Makes sense," his mother said. He shouldn't care that his mother seemed taken with Prudence, but he was. He wanted his mother to like someone he cared about. The same went for Angel. No matter what the paternity test revealed, he wanted to ensure Angel had a good home. He highly doubted that meant having anything to do with Libby's parents. She hid him from them. She hid her pregnancy.

A few dots clicked into place. Was she afraid they wouldn't approve of him?

It was probably his ego talking, looking for an excuse other than the simple fact Libby didn't love him. Crazy, because it was water under the bridge now. And yet, he wanted to know if this child had been conceived with love.

Cart before the horse, Firebrand. First, he needed to see if Angel belonged to him at all.

Looking at Prudence as she talked to his mother, his heart was making designs that it couldn't afford.

PRUDENCE LIKED MRS. FIREBRAND. The woman had a kind face, gentle disposition, and came across as a doting mother. Her hands looked like a gardener's, no polish or fake nails there. She had an earthy appeal. As far as Firebrands went, Prudence was now four-for-four. She hadn't met his father yet, and based on Adam's description, the man sounded bullheaded. She would reserve judgment until she looked him in the eyes and shook his hand.

"I've seen you in town. Now, I have a reason to speak to you," Mrs. Firebrand said with the kind of warmth that wrapped Prudence in a hug. She was caught off guard by the acknowledgment. Most folks couldn't pick her out of a lineup to say she lived in the same town.

"I'd like that a lot." Prudence held Miss Peabody a little closer. The sweet girl was shaking a little less.

Hutch got up and moseyed over, sniffing every surface along the way.

Mrs. Firebrand's eyes lit up when she looked at her son.

"The Marshall never allowed animals inside the house." Her mischievous look was endearing. "He could be such an old ninny." Her nose wrinkled when she said the last word.

"So if anyone asks, you're pet sitting in the morning. Okay?" Adam asked.

"I suppose it is true," she responded with a nonchalant shrug. And then the spark returned to her brown eyes.

"Plus, it's no one's business but ours what I'm doing at the Marshall's house."

"Believe me, I don't like putting you in a bad position. If you don't feel comfortable leaving out some of the truth, by all means go ahead—"

She waved her son off before he could finish.

"It's settled," she said, chin up. "Now, I better get back home and get to bed. Early rise in the morning."

"Thank you, Mom," Adam said with a hug and kiss on the top of her head.

She shushed him away as she took a look into the carrier. "She sure is a beautiful baby."

"True," he said and Prudence heard the pride in his tone.

She wasn't doing such a great job of protecting herself, because she had to agree with both of them. Angel was something special, all right.

Mrs. Firebrand walked to the back door. She stopped and turned. "You know about the will?"

"Brax stopped by earlier," he said.

"The men are already fighting and their father hasn't had a proper burial yet." She made the sign of the cross. "I hope you boys learn from them and don't make the same mistakes. No good ever came out of fighting for the sake of arguing."

Prudence couldn't help but be charmed by Adam's mother. It had been too long since she'd had one and this lady seemed very special.

"I do my best to get along," Adam said.

"Keep at it. The others will come around eventually," she said, before wagging her index finger in the air. "Or they'll have to live with regret."

On that note, she took her exit. The woman knew how to leave an impression.

"There's dog food on the front porch. I better—"

"I can bring it in," Adam volunteered. He was off before she could stop him. He hauled the bags into the kitchen and then set up the bowls, filling them with water. "When do they eat?"

"I should have asked Randy when the last time they were fed, but they usually eat after dinner." She thought of Mr. and Mrs. Ramsey. Again, her heart hurt for the losses that had been racking up. "They should be good until morning."

"Any medicines I need to know about?" Adam asked.

"None. They're both healthy," she said.

"We'll have to watch that one when she goes outside. Can't have a coyote nabbing her from the backyard," Adam said.

"I always go with them when they do their business. This guy here is a jumper. Not many fences are capable of holding him in. So I always have to keep an eye on him," she admitted.

"Have you considered what to do with them on a more permanent basis?" he asked.

She snuggled Miss Peabody. "I'm thinking of keeping them both. They know me and we have a good relationship. We have trust established and I know their routines. It would be an easier transition for them."

"What about your job?" His dark brow arched.

"I'll have to figure that part out," she admitted. One step at a time.

He nodded.

"Speaking of meals, when was her last bottle?" she asked.

"Hour and a half ago," he said after a quick glance at the clock and even faster mental calculation.

"Did you ever realize how often a newborn fed?" It was probably the stress of the day that made her laugh. It was either laugh or cry.

Adam cracked a smile.

"I had no idea," he said.

That statement covered so much of what had happened in the past twenty-four hours. The day should have felt like the longest in her life but there was something about being with Adam that gave her shelter in a raging storm.

"Hutch just did his business. Sorry about the front lawn," she said. "I had no way to scoop without my supplies."

"I'll get it in the morning," he said. "Besides, I'm sure there'll be others. Though we should probably keep him in the backyard from now on. It'll give him plenty of room to run and there's an invisible fence to keep critters out. The reverse will be true with him. He won't be able to cross it and escape no matter how high of a jumper he is."

"That's a relief," she said.

"We should still keep an eye on the lady, though. Coyotes can get creative when they spot an easy meal."

"They won't get this girl." She held Miss Peabody against her cheek. There'd been enough loss to last a lifetime.

And she was scared that more would happen before this investigation was over.

16

"You can take the first shower. I've got these three under control." Adam figured he could handle himself despite being sorely outnumbered.

"That's brave," Prudence shot back with a smile. At least a little bit of the ice between them was melting. "But I'll take you up on it."

She started to hand over the puffball but the little dog wasn't having it. She wiggled and stared at Adam with frightened eyes.

"I'll take her with me," Prudence said. "I can keep the shower curtain partially open and make a bed for her in the corner with a spare towel."

As she tried to leave the room, the lab followed. She tried to shoo him away but gave up after a few minutes.

"How about I set Angel up in the bedroom so the dogs will be more comfortable? I can stay until you're finished," Adam finally offered.

"Sounds like a plan." She waited on the bottom step while he lugged the baby and diaper bag upstairs. He returned for her overnight travel bag.

Standing at the top of the stairs, he signaled the troops. The minute Prudence stood up, Hutch followed. He never trusted a person who didn't get along with animals. Dogs could be some of the best judges of character.

Clearly, Prudence got the stamp of approval.

She sidestepped around him at the top of the stairs at the same moment he moved out of her way. Electricity pinged between them anytime they were near. Had his mother picked up on it earlier? She'd gone out of her way to make Prudence feel at home, which he appreciated more than words could express.

"I shouldn't be too long," Prudence said as she moved to her suitcase. She set Miss Peabody down and opened the case. The little dog took the opportunity to hop right in with the clothes.

Prudence stopped what she was doing and sat back on her heels.

"My scent must be all over the bag," she said.

Lucky dog, he thought. But said, "It probably gives her a lot of comfort to be surrounded by something so familiar."

"Well, I think we just found her new bed." Prudence pulled out a few garments and then slid the suitcase into the bathroom.

Hutch, on the other hand, hopped up on the sofa and curled up in a ball at one end. Not before digging around enough to knock a throw pillow off first.

Adam had a soft spot for animals in general. These two hit him in the place he normally kept tucked away, making him feel things he couldn't afford to feel. Things like attachment.

He managed to get Angel out of the carrier and into her crib without waking her, a feat that deserved a hushed celebration.

It was probably the day wearing on him and the news Libby was gone, but he wanted nothing more than to climb inside those sheets and sleep. Since more than a couple hour's nap would be impossible, he waited his turn with more impatience than intended.

When he heard the shower kick on, he moved over to Hutch. The lab's tail started swishing back and forth when Adam stopped and then squatted down. "You found a good home, ole' boy."

A well of emotion stirred in his chest, catching him off guard. He didn't normally do sentiment, and yet his heart went out to the dog. How could it not?

Adam pushed up and walked over to the window, staring out at the clouds that were moving at a steady clip. There weren't enough of them to promise rain, which was unfortunate. The parched earth's throat cracked from dryness and summer hadn't started yet. If the second day of June saw cracks in the soil, he could only imagine how bad things would get come August when the relentless heat kicked in.

He checked on Angel. The name fit her. His ducks were in a row for the morning and he had no idea what to expect with Libby's parents. Getting through tonight with Prudence was a whole other ballgame. He missed the closeness he felt before the wall went up. The kisses they'd shared kept replaying in his mind and were, without a doubt, the most intense he'd ever experienced. They more than hinted at mind-blowing sex...

Not something he needed to focus on when she was in the next room, naked, and in the shower. No reason to torture himself when she'd been clear. She was done with him.

THE ALARM, a.k.a. Angel, went off at four a.m.

Prudence tossed her covers off and rolled out of bed, reaching for her glasses. Thankfully, the crib was right there, and the binky quieted the little girl. She would be satisfied long enough to make a bottle of formula and change a diaper.

She glanced over at Adam's side of the bed and noticed the covers hadn't been touched. She'd gone out so hard after her shower she didn't realize he hadn't slept next to her.

"I got the bottle if you want diaper duty," his gruff, sleepy voice tugged at her heartstrings. She couldn't afford to let him get to her.

"Diaper duty it is," she said, doing her best to hide her disappointment at the sleeping arrangement. He must have taken the loveseat with Hutch.

She flipped the nightlight on and caught sight of his shirtless, muscled back as he stretched his arms out and then shrugged into a cotton t-shirt. The color black had never looked better on a person, she thought.

Miss Peabody barely looked up from the suitcase that had been strategically placed close enough to the bed for Prudence to keep watch. Lot of good it did, because the minute Prudence closed her eyes, she was out last night. Adam must have taken the midnight feeding.

How? She was scratching her head as to how that man could go days without sleep. They'd been together three nights now and he couldn't have had more than a couple of hours here and there.

Prudence needed a straight eight with no interruptions, but nine was better. She didn't even have to sleep that last hour. She liked waking up slowly, staying in bed and under the covers as long as possible before starting her day. Getting up leisurely was generally out of the question while she was working. Lazy days were made for the times in between jobs.

The diaper change took a couple of minutes. By the time she was finished, Adam had returned with the bottle. She couldn't deny they made a good team. Getting right out of bed for this kiddo was worth it.

She smelled the baby's blanket. "I expected her to be pretty rank by now."

"I gave her a sponge bath last night," Adam said.

"What? How?" She must have slept like a rock. But, really, no surprise there. Still, she felt guilty for not being there to help.

"I've had to take care of abandoned baby animals. This isn't much different," he stated.

"You've definitely gotten the hang of this..." She searched for a word other than 'parenting' and came up empty.

"Once I got over the fear that I'd break her in half on accident, I saw the similarities. I threw her clothes in the wash," he said.

"How'd you manage that?"

"Wrapped her in a towel." He smiled at the baby and Prudence could clearly see how easily he was bonding with Angel.

But then, the kid was special.

"You did great. She smells amazing and her clothes are clean," Prudence said with a little bit of awe in her voice. He deserved the praise.

"While you give her the bottle, I'll run downstairs and see what's for breakfast," he said.

"I feel like a slacker here." Prudence was only half-joking.

"You've been incredible with her," he quickly countered. "I don't know how I would have gotten through that first night without you."

The truth was that she had him to thank. She doubted she would be alive without him. Someone was after the baby, and she would have ended up collateral damage. The words got stuck in her throat, along with a few others. Words like, *I missed you last night,* and, *kiss me again,* wouldn't help her ability to keep an emotional distance from him.

The baby was another story. It was impossible not to fall for this little nugget. A little voice in the back of her mind picked that moment to tell her she'd fallen hard for Adam too. The voice was getting louder by the minute despite all her efforts to quash it.

By the time Angel finished the bottle, the dogs had been fed and taken out. Prudence brought the baby down as Adam let his mother in the backdoor.

"Good morning," she practically chirped. Her eyes sparkled when she greeted Prudence and the cheesy grin on her face gave away that she was thinking that Prudence and Adam were a couple.

Prudence hated to be the bearer of bad news…

Correcting his mother would only call more attention to their non-relationship. And she didn't have it in her heart to be the one to wipe the smile off Mrs. Firebrand's face.

"May I?" she asked, looking at Angel with such appreciation.

"Of course." Prudence handed the baby over. "I'd tell you how to take care of her, but with nine sons under your belt, you don't need a novice like me piping in."

Mrs. Firebrand's eyes lit up. "It has been a long time since I had one of these in my arms."

She seemed to bite her tongue rather than give her son a hard time for not giving her a grandbaby already. Based on Adam's tense expression, Prudence had guessed right.

"She's every four hours with a bottle of formula," Adam said to his mother. "These guys should be okay for a while. They've already been fed and let out."

"Got it," his mother said. Living on a ranch for the past forty years or so, she must know a thing or two about keeping animals.

Prudence couldn't imagine leaving Angel and the dogs in better hands.

"I dug out some old nightgowns from when you and your brothers were babies," his mother said proudly. She motioned toward the overflowing handbag hooked onto the back of a dining chair. "Don't worry. No one saw a thing."

She winked. Could this woman be any more endearing?

Prudence could easily see where Adam got his charm from. Based on everything he'd said so far, it couldn't have been his father.

"We'd better head out," Adam said. "Thank you for coming by and doing this. It means a lot."

"It's nothing," she shooed him away like he was a bothersome fly.

Prudence couldn't help but think she would miss this place when the investigation closed. And she had a feeling the end was closer than she wanted it to be.

She said her goodbyes and then reclaimed her spot on the passenger side as Adam took the driver's side. He started the engine and looked over at her like he had something important to say. He must've thought better of it because he shook his head and put the gearshift in reverse.

"In all the excitement this morning, I totally forgot my morning caffeine," she said when they were finally on the road.

"We have time to stop off," he said. "I could use a cup."

"Yes, please." She folded her arms. It had only been three days, and yet not having a baby to hold made her confused as to what she should do with her arms.

She moved her hands, placing them palms down on her thighs.

If this was what she was like after three days, she couldn't imagine how difficult separation would be after a year or two. Forget even longer.

Adam pulled off the highway and into a popular coffee chain's drive-through. Less than five minutes later, she had a steaming latte in hand. Regular coffee did the trick most days, but this was amazing.

She realized she was distracting herself thinking about the baby and coffee, rather than overthink what they might be walking into. "What do you know about Libby's parents?"

Adam rubbed the day-old scruff on his chin. He took a sip of coffee and then shrugged.

"Not much," he admitted. "Nothing from Libby. Any time I brought the subject up, she maneuvered out of answering. Last night when I couldn't sleep, I searched their names on the laptop. They seem respectable."

"Looks can be deceiving," she countered. She'd learned that lesson the hard way after going out with Chet. He'd shown up fifteen minutes early to their date. Spoke to her uncle with the utmost respect. The guy even brought flowers. He was polite to teachers, which was part of the reason she agreed to go out with him in the first place. Rather than take her straight to the movies, like he'd said, he'd pit stopped at the lake. She spent the next ten minutes fighting him off before delivering a punch that broke his nose and bloodied her new shirt. She managed to climb out the passenger's side. The car beside them took pity on her and opened the door. They were seniors, two years ahead of her and Chet. He'd sent threatening texts telling her to keep quiet about what had happened. He'd told her no one would believe her anyway.

She'd been too mortified to speak up. Until Amy Dunbar did. Four others came forward after Prudence. Her only regret was that she'd waited.

Adam didn't speak. He gripped the steering wheel so hard his knuckles turned white. He clenched his back teeth together, making his jaw muscle tick.

She held onto the cup with both hands to stop herself from reaching out to him. It would be a mistake to be his comfort, no matter how much she wanted to be.

By the time she finished her latte, Adam was pulling into the parking lot at the sheriff's office.

The two-story building was nondescript, brown bricks with tall, thin windows.

Adam drained his coffee before issuing a sharp sigh. He stared at the bottom of the cup.

"Here goes nothing," he said, opening his door. His words might have been meant to be breezy but they were anything but. Angel's grandparents would soon follow. They had rights.

The right to take her away?

17

The witness room, as Lawler had called it, wasn't much more than the size of a broom closet. It had the same long length and short width. If Adam turned sideways and extended his arms, he'd be touching wall-to-window.

The room was dimly lit and there were four metal fold-up chairs a foot away that faced the window. Adam had to pull a chair back a couple of feet to fit. He'd been quiet on the way in. Meeting Libby's parents for the first time was messing with his head.

The very real possibility they could take their grandchild away before the paternity test came back was a hot poker to his chest. If he had to get a lawyer and fight to stop it from happening, he wouldn't think twice. The family lawyer would have contacts in the adoption arena.

If Libby hid her baby from her parents, she had to have had a good reason. Doubts crept in at how well he'd actually known his ex-girlfriend, though. She never mentioned anything about coming from money. Based on the society page pictures he'd seen last night, her family had to be doing well.

Tension and frustration caused the spot between his shoulder blades to act up. He rolled his shoulders a couple of times in an attempt to ease the strain.

Prudence scooted her chair closer to his. She reached over to him, and he took her hand, clasping their fingers together. One look at her said she was mulling over the same possibility and didn't like it any more than he did.

"I don't care who they are," she said under her breath. "We won't let them take her."

"The law might see it differently," he said. He didn't have any plans to turn Angel over to strangers.

"Then, it's our job to make them understand."

He squeezed her hand as a couple walked into the adjacent room. They both had on suits. Mrs. Warrington's came with a skirt. She had on navy blue while Mr. Warrington wore a steel gray. They were put together in a crisp, corporate look. Not a hair was out of place on Mrs. Warrington and her oversized pearls were the right compliment to soften her look.

Libby had been the perfect mix of her parents. Her father's sun-kissed skin. Her mother's flawless complexion. Her father's blond hair and her mother's oval face. They had the kind of bodies that came from a gym or yoga class, maybe both.

"They look awfully put together for people who just found out their daughter was murdered," Prudence whispered.

"I was just thinking the same thing," he admitted.

The only tell was when they turned to face the mirror. There were dark circles under Mr. Warrington's eyes. Mrs. Warrington dabbed hers with a delicate white handkerchief.

Lawler instructed them to sit down, which they did.

When Mrs. Warrington sat down, she put her face in her hands and it was like someone had let the air out of a balloon. Her husband placed an arm around her shoulders to comfort her.

"This is a very difficult time for our family. Please make this brief," Mr. Warrington said.

"I'll do everything I can to keep this brief." Lawler's back was to the window and his heft blocked some of Adam's view.

Mrs. Warrington shuddered before sitting up again. When she did, he expected to see mascara smudges on her cheeks. Her makeup was flawless.

Lawler launched into a sincere monologue of how sorry he was for their loss before asking his first question.

"When were you notified of your daughter's murder?" he asked.

Mrs. Warrington blew her nose in her hanky. She tucked it away after that and took in a breath. Of the two of them, she seemed to be taking the news the hardest. Her husband's back was stiff and he immediately retracted his arm once she seemed able to go on.

"I can't remember much of anything," Mrs. Warrington said. "I'm afraid I won't be any good to you."

"We were notified the morning before yesterday." Mr. Warrington stared at the ceiling where it met the wall in the corner of the room. His chin quivered but he pulled it together, glancing down at his slacks and picking imaginary lint off them.

His wife nodded but didn't look up.

Despite their chilly exterior, it was easy to see they cared about what happened to their daughter.

Lawler asked a few routine-sounding questions.

"Is it strange to you they've been here..." Prudence glanced at the clock on the wall, "fifteen minutes already and have yet to ask about their granddaughter?"

"As a matter of fact, I was just about to make the same observation." He'd noted their lack of interest.

"I'd like to thank you for coming here so early this morning," Lawler seemed ready to wrap the interview up.

"What about the child?" Mr. Warrington finally asked. He leaned forward like he was about to divulge a secret. "Is it possible to keep it out of the news?"

"It?" Prudence's disgust mirrored his own.

"I mean, none of our friends know and I can't see any reason for this situation to come to light," Mr. Warrington continued. "No good could come from it."

Adam wished he could see Lawler's face right about then.

"Is it safe to say, then, you want nothing to do with your granddaughter?" Lawler asked, his voice a study in calm. It dawned on Adam that a man in Lawler's line of work probably saw and heard just about everything.

"We aren't saying that exactly," Mr. Warrington hemmed.

"This would be a good time for a grandmother to step in and shut her husband up," Prudence whispered.

"Is it wrong that I'd rather they not want to be involved?" Adam would do whatever was best for Angel. Still, he figured she was far better off without those cold-hearted people. He still couldn't get over the fact Mr. Warrington had called his own grandchild an "it."

"No. They make my skin crawl just looking at them," Prudence admitted. "I don't want them anywhere near our Angel."

She squeezed his hand as she studied the couple on the

other side of the mirror. Did she realize she'd just called Angel theirs?

Stranger yet, his heart didn't protest.

He'd never felt this way about another person, not even Libby and he'd been intent on marrying her. He realized now that she'd done him a favor in walking away, but he stopped short of calling Angel a mistake. If the child belonged to him, he planned to give her everything she deserved. If she didn't, he intended to make certain her father did.

The thought occurred to him Libby might have been on the run from Angel's birth father. The paternity test would tell. Waiting for the results, not knowing when so many lives hung in the balance was the worst.

After seeing Libby's parents in action, he now understood why she kept the pregnancy from them. If they didn't want anything to do with their dead daughter's child, they weren't worth her time.

"I can't promise the news won't connect the dots or run their own investigation," Lawler said, his voice flat. He rarely gave his mood away. So, Adam was surprised at how much his tone changed toward the Warringtons.

"I've seen enough. Should we head out before these jerks leave?" Adam said to Prudence. They'd been away from the house for an hour and a half already. His mother hadn't called or texted, so that was a good sign.

"They aren't worth our time, let alone hers." Prudence stood up.

Without any fanfare, they exited the building. In the parking lot, Adam noticed a man in a suit who was leaning against the opened door of his truck and smoking a cigarette. From this distance, he looked to be in his late thirties and had a runner's build. He had sandy-blond hair that had a deep part on one side and was combed over the front. His crisp suit gave him an air of importance. Businessman? Lawyer?

The second made more sense outside of a sheriff's office. So, why was he trying to cover the fact he watched every step Prudence took?

∾

A CHILL RACED down Prudence's spine, like the sensation people referred to when they said a cat walked over their grave. She scanned the parking lot, her gaze stopping on a man in a suit three rows over.

"Do you know who that is?" she asked Adam.

"Never seen him before in my life," Adam confirmed.

"Something about him gives me the creeps," she admitted. "I can't put a finger on it, though."

"He seems a little too interested in you." Anger laced Adam's voice. "I'll make sure he doesn't follow us."

Prudence climbed inside the cab of the truck. She touched Adam's arm after he took the driver's seat. "Maybe we should see if he does first."

Adam stared at the rearview for a long moment.

"You're right. Let's see if he takes the bait." He started the engine and put the gearshift in reverse.

As he was backing out of the spot, Prudence noticed the Warringtons leaving the sheriff's office.

"Hey, check that out." She motioned toward them.

Adam followed along.

"If I head toward them with my foot on the pedal, do me a favor. Grab the wheel," he said. There was a hint of truth in that statement. He wouldn't do anything to put himself in legal jeopardy, but she didn't blame him for having half a mind to run them over.

"They'll never know how special she is," Prudence said. Her own parents had been taken from her. The idea of family willingly walking away from something so small and so precious was something she could scarcely fathom.

"Their loss," he said.

"I couldn't agree more." Was there a way to make the arrangement permanent? Have them relinquish any rights to Angel in case they changed their minds in a couple of years?

Based on how detached they were from anything to do with Angel, she highly doubted it. But better safe than sorry. Everything about that little girl's future hung in the balance pending the results of the paternity test.

Adam had the resolve and the means to care for Angel in the manner she deserved. What if he wasn't the father? What if his ex had met someone else? What if she was on the run or in hiding? There were so many unanswered questions in this case.

It had only been three days, the voice in the back of her mind reminded.

She glanced in the side-view mirror. Panic washed over her, squeezing her chest. Why did the suit seem familiar?

"I half expected the Warringtons to go talk to the mystery man," Prudence said.

"The fact they don't seem to know each other raises some concern," he admitted. "I'm more interested in your reaction to him, though. They could be putting on a show to throw off anyone who might be watching."

"Right." She kept an eye on the suit.

Adam turned on his blinker. He stopped at the corner. He hesitated. Then, he made a left.

"Let me just make a U-turn here and we'll see if the suit follows," Adam said. He used a side parking lot to make the U, then pulled onto the side of the road. He drove down the road a piece before making a few more turns.

Sure enough, the suit followed. He stopped the minute he saw the trap, put the gearshift in reverse, and gunned it.

Tires burned on the concrete road as they struggled for purchase. They caught and the truck whirled backward. Adam wasted no time peeling rubber to catch up to the suit.

"Grab my phone and take a picture of the driver. I'll get as close as I can," he stated. All his focus was on the vehicle in front of him.

Prudence fumbled for his phone. Her hand shook from a shot of adrenaline and nerves. She managed to grab it, and steady her hand enough to take a couple of shots. The sun was up, and the truck swerved, so she had no idea if she was getting anything usable.

"I hope I got something," she said.

Just then the truck slammed on its brakes. Adam reacted but the second cost him. He ran straight into the vehicle in front.

Prudence's head snapped forward and then back against the headrest. Airbags deployed, blocking her view. It was probably a good thing because the windshield cracked, and slivers of glass showered the bags.

Everything happened so fast at that point.

In the next second, a man was at her door. He got hold of the handle before she had time to hit the lock button. She grabbed onto her armrest and held on for dear life.

At this distance, she could clearly see the suit's face as he practically sneered at her. He had a scar on his right cheekbone, a streak of white on an overly tanned face. His steel eyes were like a snake's.

Her body revolted against him, and she knew why.

He'd been there when she'd picked up a frantic hitch-hiker, a desperate woman clutching a baby to her chest.

"It's him," Prudence whispered as shock and disbelief gave way to white-hot anger. Anger for the life he took. Anger for the child he tried to rip from her arms. Anger for a child who would never know her mother.

As the suit tried to wrestle the baby out of Prudence's arms, Libby's face appeared behind him. Her arms raised up high and Prudence saw the sharp boulder moments before it had struck.

His head had snapped forward, and then he'd spun around.

"Go," Libby had demanded. "Keep her safe. I'll find you."

The memories flooded Prudence as she struggled to maintain her grip on the armrest.

18

J ust as her fingers were about to give, the suit spun around. The next thing Prudence knew, his back slammed up against her door. She hit the lock button and scrambled to get out from the driver's side as Adam threw a punch so hard the man's head snapped to the right.

She ran her hand along the floorboard, searching for a weapon. Bingo. She curled her fingers around a handle and then pulled out a hammer.

As she rounded the back of the truck, she caught sight of blood.

The next few moments happened in slow motion.

Adam threw a punch so hard she heard the suit's jaw snap. She was certain he'd broken bone. As Adam brought his fist up for another round, blood squirted from his hand. A lot of blood.

She glanced around for some kind of weapon. A knife?

The glint of metal five feet behind Adam caught her eye. Suit must've found it at the same time because he lunged toward Adam, using the truck to deliver enough force to knock Adam back a couple of steps.

As the suit dropped to the ground, Prudence dove toward the knife. She knocked it farther away half a second before the suit got there. Her skin burned where the concrete shredded her forearm as she landed. She managed to keep her head from slamming into the pavement.

But the suit gripped her by the chin, squeezing until she thought her eyeballs might pop out.

"Where's the kid?" he ground out.

With all her strength, she slammed the hammer into his forehead as Adam literally pulled the man off her. The suit went flying up, hands behind his back as Adam put him in some type of wrestling lock.

The suit's head snapped back, and he blinked a few times like he was barely holding onto consciousness.

The sweet sound of sirens split the air. Help was coming.

Still, she scrambled toward the knife and kicked it as far as she could. The sound of metal grinding across concrete caused her shoulders to tense.

"You'll never find her," Adam said, hauling the suit chest first over the hood of the pickup truck.

"They will." Adrenaline must have kicked in, giving the lawyer a boost to stay coherent. Blood splattered from his nose and colored his teeth in what looked like red dye.

Who would? The grandparents? Her main concern right now was Adam. Blood dripped from his elbow. There was a lot. Too much.

Lawler's SUV roared up to the scene. He was out of the driver's seat and handcuffing the suit faster than Prudence could say, under arrest.

"I'm a lawyer," the suit claimed. "I'll sue the shirt off this department if I'm not provided emergency medical care now."

Lawler quickly assessed the scene.

"You'll have access to medicine," he said. Right now, though, I plan to read your rights." He walked the lawyer over to the back of the SUV and moved him inside as he started with, "You have the right to remain silent..."

Prudence hopped to her feet and ran to Adam. Lawler was there. The lawyer was going to jail. The news seemed to sink in as he confessed that he'd been hired by the Warringtons to make 'the little problem' go away.

Would they sign over their rights and walk away now? They wouldn't need to. She overheard Lawler making the call to his office to place them both under arrest.

She skimmed Adam, looking for signs of injury. Her gaze stopped on his arm where blood pulsed out of his wound. "You're hurt."

"It's a scratch. I need something to tie it off with," he said. "Stop the bleeding."

She immediately found a towel in his backseat.

He tied off his arm above the wound, which stemmed the bleeding while an ambulance pulled up, and a pair EMTs came bolting toward them.

"Let's have a look at that injury, sir," one of them said. He was young, early twenties if Prudence had to guess. All she could think of was how easily it would have been to lose Adam today. The thought gutted her. Her heart squeezed because in that instant, she saw a different future unfold. One where he was gone and her life was empty.

She couldn't allow that to happen, not without fighting for the future she wanted. Needed?

Yes, she needed Adam in her life and she had to know if he felt the same.

An EMT went to work on him, but he tried to wave him off.

"She's injured," Adam said. "You can work on me when I know she's all right."

"It's barely a scratch," she said. Her skin burned but she was nowhere near as badly injured as he was. "It's no worse than playing hopscotch on the playground and taking a fall."

Adam locked gazes with her and her heart free fell. Butterflies released in her stomach.

"Will you let him finish his job if I come over there?" she asked.

"We can talk about it," he said.

She walked over to him on his good side and reached for his hand. She told the EMT to go ahead and warned Adam that if he argued she would find a way to make him regret it later.

"Will there be a later?" he asked, with the most sincere look in those perfect eyes of his.

"There will if I have anything to say about it," she reassured.

Adam leaned over and pressed a tender kiss to her lips. "I was hoping you'd say something like that."

"I hate to interrupt, but we need to take you for a ride," the EMT said.

"I've nursed back worse injuries with antibiotic ointment and field stitches." Adam tried to blow the young guy off.

"How about I go with you?" Prudence asked, tugging on his hand. She caught his gaze and held it. "I need you in tiptop form later."

Mischief danced in his eyes when he said, "You heard the lady. We're going to the ER."

"Don't let these stitches hold you back from whatever you planned to do to me later." Adam winked at Prudence as she took the driver's seat of a ranch truck brought to them by Brax.

She leaned across the cab and kissed him.

Not even the pain medication he was on could dull his senses enough to stop his body from reacting to her soft, full lips pressed against his. He'd been wanting to kiss her all day.

Prudence pulled back first. "Remind me to finish that later."

"Now's a good time," he teased. He was only half joking.

She laughed.

"I'll keep that in mind. But someone has to drive this thing," she said.

He held back the remark that was ready on his tongue.

"Plus, the doctor ordered rest. You aren't supposed to get too excited. Remember?" she asked.

"I was hoping you weren't listening to that part," he admitted with another grin.

"We have all the time we want, Adam. There's no reason to rush," she said as she started backing out of the parking spot.

"Do you mean that?" he asked.

She stopped the truck half-in and half-out and put the gearshift in park.

"Yes, I do." She kept her gaze straight ahead.

His seatbelt was off in a heartbeat and he practically flew across the seat.

"I know it's only been three days, but when I met you my whole life flashed before my eyes. I used to think love at first sight was nothing more than hormones but now I know different," he started, searching for the right words to let her know just how hard he'd fallen for her.

She met his gaze, her eyes were wide, and he saw so much emotion behind those beautiful blues. Her thick glasses couldn't hide the beauty there. "The same thing happened to me, like a lightning bolt."

"I don't know if I'm Angel's father but I already feel like we're supposed to be a family. Together. The three of us," he continued.

"Couldn't have said it better myself, Adam," she said. "What do we do with it, though?"

"Make a commitment right here and now," he said without hesitation. Knowing she'd felt that same jolt when they'd met spurred him on. "I have fallen in love with you. Hard." He saw the glittery need in her eyes. "I've been around a long time and dated more people than I care to count trying to find something missing in my life. Turns out, nothing was. I'm whole. You're whole. And I'm a whole lot better when you're with me. What I'm saying is that I love you, Prudence."

She brought her hand up to cover a gasp. And then she studied him. *Really* studied him.

A wide smile broke out on her face as she dropped her hand.

"I love you too, Adam. And I can't imagine ever loving anyone more," she said.

"It's crazy because I thought I missed my chance. That love and a family was going to work out fine for my brothers. But because I waited, I thought I'd somehow missed my chance," he said. "Until you came along. And then I realized why it had never been right before. Because I hadn't met you."

"That's the sweetest thing anyone's ever said to me before, Adam Firebrand."

"Then make me the happiest person in the world."

She gasped a second time as he reached for her hand, taking it in his, and he could feel hers trembling ever so slightly. "Marry me, Prudence. Allow me to spend the rest of our lives getting to know you and proving to you every day that you made the right choice."

Now it was his turn to be nervous. It was a strange sensation. One he'd never felt before. And yet, with Prudence he figured there was so much more to explore.

"Yes," she said instantly. "I'll marry you, Adam. I've never been in love with anyone like I love you. And whether Angel turns out to be ours or not, she'll always be part of our family."

Adam kissed his future bride, his love, his life.

And one word came to mind...*home.*

A horn honked, breaking into the moment. Prudence pulled back and laughed. Mischief danced in her eyes— eyes that he couldn't wait to spend the rest of his life staring into.

She shifted into reverse and then made her way to the exit.

"Miss Peabody and Hutch will make great additions to the main house," Adam said. "My cabin isn't big enough for all five of us."

"Will your family be okay with us moving in like that?" she asked.

"You saw how few people were willing to go inside now that the Marshall is gone. I imagine we won't get too much blow-back if we go through the right channels," he said. "Besides, the only time that place has ever felt like home has been with you, Angel, and the dogs in it. It's time for a change around Firebrand Ranch."

Change was inevitable. In this case, it was time to breathe new life into the old place. And he figured his father and uncle had bigger battles to fight.

"I love it there," Prudence said and that was all he needed to hear.

"Then, we'll start moving in tonight," he said.

"What if she..."

She couldn't seem to finish her sentence, but he knew exactly what she was going to say.

"We'll cross that bridge when we come to it," he said. "Either way, we'll find a way to have her as part of our lives."

"You knew her mother best. It's important to keep her memory alive," Prudence said from a voice of experience. "We never talked about my parents or my sister after the murders."

"That's a done deal," he said without hesitation. He absolutely planned to ensure that Libby's memory was alive and well for Angel. "Do you have any pictures of your family to put up in our new house?"

He hadn't seen any at Prudence's home.

"In a box in the attic," she admitted. "I'm not sure why I never took them out."

"It probably never occurred to you once they were packed away," he said.

"Then, by all means, let's bring them out." Her voice sounded lighter, like the burden she'd been carrying for too many years was lifting.

Adam liked being part of the reason.

"I wouldn't be against trying to add to the crew when that arm heals," she said, more of that mischief in her tone.

"Somehow, I foresee a lot of practice in our future," he teased.

"I'm counting on it," she said as she pulled up to their new home at Firebrand.

Adam made it out of the passenger seat in time to open her door. He kissed her again for good measure before linking their hands and heading into their new home.

The smell of food wafted down the hallway as they entered the house.

"In all the excitement, I forgot all about eating until right now," Prudence groaned. "I'm starving."

"The medicine is dulling my appetite but I could eat," he admitted, needing to see Angel.

They were greeted by Hutch first with Miss Peabody on his heels.

Prudence bent down to pick up Miss Peabody, who was so excited she was shaking. Hutch nearly knocked Prudence on her backside as he plowed into her.

"Sit," she commanded.

He did. Adam was still impressed by that trick.

But his heart wasn't full until he saw their angel. His mother brought a smiling, content baby to them, meeting them halfway down the hall.

Her gaze immediately flew to the patch on his arm.

"I'm so glad you called to tell me what happened to you. I'm still shocked and I knew it was coming," she said, concern evident in her voice.

"It's not much more than a scratch," he said, trying to wave it off like it was nothing.

"That settles it. I'm staying until you're up and around again," she said.

He stretched his arms out. He showed her flat palms.

The last part might have made him wince, but he was a fast healer.

"How did it go at the sheriff's office?" she asked, and then added, "Come in first. How rude of me. I thought you might be hungry, so I made meatballs."

Adam decided not to ask how she'd managed to care for the dogs, take care of a newborn and find the time to make meatballs. Mothers were amazing creatures.

"I thought there might be a legal battle for her with the grandparents. Turns out they don't want anything to do with her," Adam said.

His mother whirled around.

"Are they crazy? Or just stupid and mean?" She didn't bother hiding her shock.

"All three if you ask me," Prudence said under her breath.

His mother mumbled something in Italian that he probably didn't want to understand.

"What about the parents?" she asked.

"You might be looking at them." Adam didn't go into detail. He didn't have to. His mother shot him a look that said she was proud of him for stepping up.

"If her grandparents are willing to sign away their rights," she started in a conspiratorial tone. "I know someone who can play around with her birth certificate."

Shock didn't begin to cover Adam's reaction to his normally straight-laced, by-the-book mother's statement.

"What you're suggesting is illegal," he countered.

"It's fudging," she said like it was no big deal. But an emotion danced behind her eyes that he couldn't quite put his finger on. "No one has to know."

Adam took a minute to let that sink in.

"Besides, I already can see you would go to the ends of

the earth for this child. It's nothing a loving parent wouldn't do to protect their baby," she said like she was done talking about it. She went over to the pot of meatballs and stirred.

End of subject.

Adam made a note to ask more about those statements later. Right now, he didn't want to break the celebratory mood.

"I have other news." He looked to Prudence for approval.

She nodded, her smile so big and so warm it could light a hundred campfires.

"Oh yeah?" That got his mother's attention.

"Prudence agreed to do me the honor of marrying me," he said as pride filled his chest. There was something else there too. Love, and a sense of home he'd never known before.

His mother's scream startled the baby.

"I cannot tell you how long I've waited to have another girl in the family," she said as she ran around the island and managed to wrap Prudence in a one-arm hug.

"I love your son with all my heart. And I can't wait to be part of this family," Prudence said, and he could tell by the look in her eyes she meant every word.

As he glanced at the baby, he realized that he could hardly wait to make their family official.

His Prudence. His future. His home.

"I can't believe you're actually a father," Brax said to his brother Adam.

"Believe me, the news is still sinking in. But I couldn't be happier about it." Adam's grin was ear-to-ear, so Brax didn't doubt it one bit.

"And now you're about to get married after swearing off the institution a few months back," Brax continued. Times were definitely changing.

"To the most incredible person in the world if I do say so myself," Adam practically beamed.

"I wouldn't argue how happy the two of you are together. Lovesick puppies with a new baby to boot." Brax smirked. "One down. Seventeen to go."

Adam laughed out loud as he jiggered with his bowtie.

"Somehow, I doubt the rest of the Firebrands will be at the altar anytime soon," Adam said. "I could barely get half the family to show up today."

"The tension about the will isn't helping," Brax said before adding, "what's the hurry about tying the knot, though?"

"When you find the person you want to spend the rest of your life with and you know with one hundred percent certainty in your heart that she's the one...there's no reason to wait," Adam said.

Brax couldn't relate. But then, he'd never fallen so head over heal in love for anyone.

"Don't get me wrong, I love that some of my family will be around to witness. But all I truly need is Prudence, the baby, and my best man," Adam continued like what was happening was perfectly normal.

Strange, because Brax figured his older brother would be the last one at the altar, especially after what happened with Libby. She'd never been right for Adam, and Brax had never once seen his brother look at Libby in the same way he did Prudence.

But the former relationship gave him one perfect daughter and that was something to behold.

Brax tugged at the collar of his shirt, thinking it was a little too tight for his liking.

"Why can't people get married in jeans and a t-shirt?" he complained.

"I doubt any guy would object to that," Adam laughed.

Their mother burst through the door at that exact moment, as if on cue. Angel was in her grandmother's arms.

"You both look very handsome. Good job," she said proudly as she stood back and took them both in.

Their mother had been acting odd lately, but not today. Today, she beamed with pride. Or, at least, she did when she looked at Adam. Another emotion Brax couldn't quite pinpoint was present when she looked at him.

Adam caught Brax's attention. He made eyes before dusting imaginary lint off his jacket. His brother acknowledged the reference to their conversation before their mother had walked in. Yes, mothers were most likely the reason guys didn't show up to their wedding day in anything but a tuxedo.

And Brax had no plans to put on one of these for himself anytime soon.

To FIND out if Brax continues to hold out once he's reunited with a special someone from the past, click here.

ALSO BY BARB HAN

Texas Firebrand

Rancher to the Rescue

Disarming the Rancher

Rancher under Fire

Rancher on the Line

Undercover with the Rancher

Rancher in Danger

Don't Mess With Texas Cowboys

Texas Cowboy's Protection (*FREE*)

Texas Cowboy Justice

Texas Cowboy's Honor

Texas Cowboy Daddy

Texas Cowboy's Baby

Texas Cowboy's Bride

Texas Cowboy's Family

Cowboys of Cattle Cove

Cowboy Reckoning (*FREE*)

Cowboy Cover-up

Cowboy Retribution

Cowboy Judgment

Cowboy Conspiracy

Cowboy Rescue

ABOUT THE AUTHOR

Barb Han is a USA TODAY and Publisher's Weekly Best-selling Author. Reviewers have called her books "heartfelt" and "exciting."

Barb lives in Texas—her true north—with her adventurous family, a poodle mix and a spunky rescue who is often referred to as a hot mess. She is the proud owner of too many books (if there is such a thing). When not writing, she can be found exploring Manhattan, on a mountain either hiking or skiing depending on the season, or swimming in her own backyard.

Sign up for Barb's newsletter at www.BarbHan.com.

Printed in Great Britain
by Amazon